I0574399

Firefly: A Lancaster Novel
Book 2
Stacy Goforth

STACY GOFORTH
author

Stacy Goforth

Library of Congress Control Number: 2025909442

Paperback ISBN: 979-8-9985002-3-7

eBook ISBN: 979-8-9985002-4-4

Book Design: by Stacy Goforth

First edition 2025

<u>Praise for the Lancaster Series: Dragonfly: Book 1</u>

Reviewed by Mimie Odigwe for Readers' Favorite

With small-town shenanigans, a tight-knit, albeit meddling family, spiteful exes, and a tender and warming love declaration at the end, I can picture Dragonfly by Stacy Goforth as a Hallmark movie. It's like Goforth knew how engrossing her book was, so there will be other books featuring the whole clan. Yay! The side characters are supportive, humorous, and have believable development. My favorites have to be Jax, Sam's perceptive and wry eldest brother, and the sassy, unfiltered Kelley, Blake's younger sister. Dragonfly isn't all fluff and flirtations; it explores how different families react to grief, the sacrifices made for family, and with just the right amount of romantic tension to keep pages turning well past bedtime. Dragonfly is for lovers of heart and heat, and anyone who has never really gotten over their crush.

To all the writers in the Captain Swan fandom who inspired me along the way. Crack on ladies, no one does enemies to lovers better than you, mates. Ahoy, lovelies, I learned from the best.

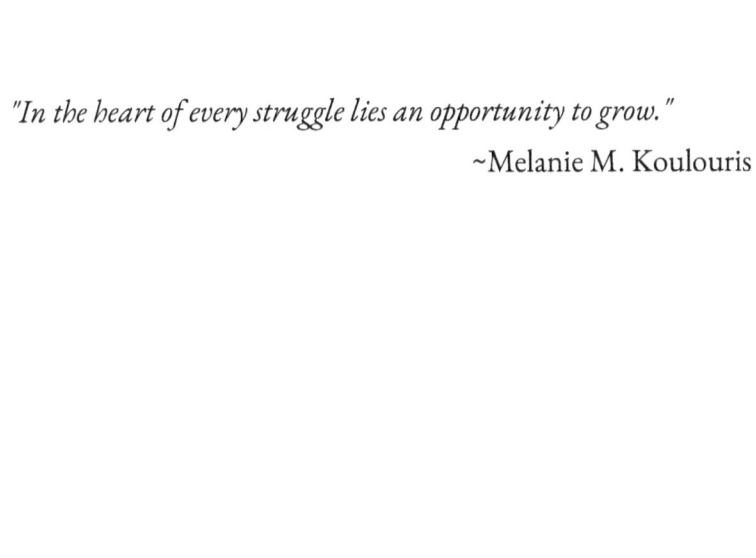

"In the heart of every struggle lies an opportunity to grow."

~Melanie M. Koulouris

The Man — Taylor Swift   3:10

Cherry Pie — Warrant   3:21

You Give Love a Bad Name — Bon Jovi   3:43

Nightmare — Halsey   3:52

Here I Go Again — Whitesnake   4:36

Boys 'Round Here — Blake Shelton/Pistol Annies   4:49

This Could Be the Night — Loverboy   4:58

Stick Season — Noah Kahan   3:02

Poison — Alice Cooper   4:30

Iris — Goo Goo Dolls   4:50

Nothin' But A Good Time — Poison   3:43

Little Lies — Fleetwood Mac   3:38

Along Comes a Woman — Chicago   4:15

The Bones — Maren Morris/Hozier   3:17

Firefly — Ed Sheeran   4:15

Dicktionary

Here for the smut? Skip this page and read on...

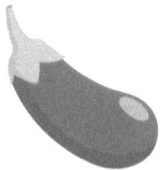

Feeling shy? Feel the need to skip through the more steamy scenes? Below is a list of chapters with sexual content so you are aware ahead of time:

Chapter Eleven

Chapter Thirteen

Chapter Fifteen

Chapter Seventeen

Chapter Twenty Six

Happy reading...

Chapter One

Jackson

Jackson was not the smartest of the Lancaster siblings. Though he would admit he was the slowest since his accident last year, but there was one thing that he excelled at that neither his sister Samantha nor his brother Dylan could ever. He could sniff out bullshit from any distance. And right now, things smelled pretty damn foul on the other end of the line as his father fed him some rancid story about sending him "help" to learn the auto shop's finances.

He had spent over a month hospitalized after a motorcycle accident had left him unable to walk. His recovery process involved the whole family, with Samantha coming back from Pittsburgh to support him and assist in his rehabilitation and Dylan covering all the shifts at the shop. Jackson spent a fair amount of his time learning how to walk again, which made him feel like a goddamn toddler.

It had been a humbling and challenging experience, though he reasoned he should be grateful that during his downtime, his younger sister had convinced their father to sell him the family business, Lancaster's Auto Shop. With his dad now free from his responsibilities, he had embarked on a nomadic journey across America in an RV, seeking self-discovery and engaging in small talk with elderly campers, clutching their yarn and beer while they gossiped by a campfire.

It seemed like a miserable existence to him, but who was he to judge what makes a man happy? *You do you, Dad!*

His current office was giving off the vibes of a bomb explosion. With paperwork spread out around him, threatening his sanity, he tried to think positively as he responded to his father on the other end of the line. "You know, Dad, I think I can get this all figured out on my own." He heard Dylan's snicker across the garage and shot him a dirty look.

"And how long will that take, Jax? Just accept the help." Despite his father's insistence, they were cut from the same stubborn cloth, and he knew that neither of them was backing down today.

"Yeah, fine, whatever. Just have the guy call me or something," he agreed, hoping that would be enough to at least end the conversation. "I'll check my schedule and see what I can do."

The chuckle on the other end of the line annoyed him, as it only meant that dear ole Dad was going to do whatever he wanted, anyway. "Yeah, Jax, I'll do that."

"I gotta go. A customer just walked in." He looked up at the empty shop. Dylan stared back at him as he glanced around and shook his head with a condescending snort. "I'll talk to you next week." He hung up the phone and groaned, rubbing his palm against his face.

"Smooth," Dylan said with a sarcastic nod. "Sounds like you handled him well."

"Go to hell." He gripped his dirty blond hair, staring at the paperwork strewn about his desk, and swirled the mouse in his hand as the black screen came back to life. A picture of his sister Samantha and her boyfriend Blake flashing him the bird, popped up on the monitor. "I need these numbers to make sense before Dad gets involved and sends some city slicker suit down here to screw up my life."

"How exactly are you going to do that?" his brother asked, wiping the grease from his forehead with the back of his hand and dropping his screwdriver into the toolbox. "Neither of us even went to city college, man. I have no clue what any of that fancy shit means."

"How hard can it be?" he said, pushing his reading glasses up onto the bridge of his nose. "Dad did it on his own all these years. It can't be that difficult."

"You know, all this time I thought Sam was stubborn, but I think you have her beat." His brother's words were dumb as hell. His sister might be stubborn, but no one was as stubborn as him, and that was an undisputed fact.

He plucked at the keyboard, one finger at a time, his tongue hanging precariously from his mouth, as he tried to enter the purchases for the week. However, the computer kept emitting an awful sound every time he hit the enter key. He knew he could figure out the damn information if given enough time. He wasn't a complete idiot, but the computer was determined to be his mortal enemy.

"Why does it keep doing that?" He smashed his fist into the keyboard angrily.

Dylan was turning off the lights over the main bay, leaving only a blue Chevy Silverado sitting in the shop that was waiting on parts that wouldn't be arriving until next week. "That's it. Time to get out of here before we need to buy a new computer," Jax growled, ignoring his brother and smashing his fingers against the keys. More lights extinguished in the garage as Dylan proceeded to shut things down. "And without even understanding any of that shit, I know we can't afford to buy a new one of those."

"Fine!" Jax said in a frustrated tone. "I need a beer, anyway." He punched his finger against the button on the monitor, causing the screen to turn black. The room was now illuminated only by the soft glow of moonlight streaming through the windows. "You going to Boondocks?" he asked, already knowing the answer.

"Yup." His brother shook his head. "You want me to drive?"

Jax limped slightly, feeling the pain in his hip, an ache in his knee, cursing as he caught up to his brother at the door. He glanced over at the motorcycle in the corner, the unfinished project he was working on to replace the bike he had lost in the crash last year, various pieces still stacked precariously in the corner that he had yet to assemble. He sighed and followed Dylan out of the garage. "Yeah, we can take the truck." He tossed the keys at his little brother and shut the door behind him.

The local bar, Boondocks, was bustling with activity for a Thursday night. One might say that it was because it was really the only joint in town where you could drink a beer and watch a game without getting hassled by someone asking about your day. Jax, who hated being hassled by anyone, sat as far back as possible when he arrived at the old bar. He slid into the corner, propped his foot up onto the wooden booth, and patiently waited for Dylan to arrive with his beer.

The Pirates game was playing on the television, and Dylan returned just in time for Casey Anderson to trot out to the pitcher's mound. Jax gestured toward the screen. "How do you feel about his multi-million dollar contract this year?"

Dylan chuckled, not bothering to look at the television. "Like it was worth a million dollars just to punch him in the face."

Jax snorted, recalling the fight that Dylan and his best friend Blake Forrester had with Casey right here in this bar last year over their sister, Sam.

Jax tipped back his beer. "I'm surprised he didn't come back and sign the goddamn menu or something." It had been front page news, having a professional ballplayer as popular as Casey Anderson stir up a bar fight in their own little town. Dylan had become somewhat of a reluctant town celebrity for months after the story broke. Jax still thought they were all idiots, but Casey *had* insulted his sister, and in Jax's book, no one dissed a lady without taking at least one to the face. Without looking up, Dylan pointed behind him to a stool at the bar. Jax shook his head with a snort. "He didn't?"

Dylan took a sip of his beer, a slight smirk on his face. "Second stool at the bar. Asshole signed his goddamn name under it. Cocky motherfucker, I'll give him that much."

"That guy really was a dumbass," Jax mused out loud. "I honestly don't know what Sam saw in him." Shaking his head, he took another sip of his beer and sighed.

Dylan scoffed. "You really gotta ask that question? She's our sister, and I don't want to think about that kind of stuff when thinking about our sister. I have a hard enough time dealing with her and Blake when I call New York." He shook his head, letting out a groan. "I swear, the two of them go at it like rabbits. If he wasn't my best friend, I would..." His voice trailed off, the unfinished thought hanging in the air.

"Admit it, bro. We lucked out with Blake," Jax said, trying to lighten the mood. Jax looked up from his beer just in time to witness a batter hit a home run off of Casey's fastball. He muttered,

"Home run, asshole," before refocusing on his brother. "Blake and Sam are kismet. Admit it, they were just meant to be."

Dylan seemed even more frustrated. "Yeah, and where does that leave me? Stuck in this goddamn town, without my best friend. My sister's too busy being happy, and I don't want to ruin that with my bullshit."

"Jesus, Dyl, you make it sound like I keep you locked in the basement with no sunshine," Jax said, glancing toward the bar. Donna Draper and her friends walked in, disrupting his attempt to lighten the mood. *Was no place sacred in this town?* "Your walking, talking distraction just arrived," he grunted.

Dylan followed Jax's gaze and frowned. "Let it go."

"I don't get what you're doing messing around with her after all the shit she pulled with Sam last year. What do you even have in common to talk about?"

Dylan took a long drink of his beer, glancing over at Donna's group. "Talking isn't exactly part of our relationship." He paused. "Unless you count all the damn questions she asks me about Blake."

"She's not even that hot, bro," Jax said. Just the thought of touching Donna Draper repulsed him. The woman was a remorseless, manipulative, trash stirrer. "Honestly, she's not worth your time."

His brother stood up from the booth, staring down at his empty beer. "You want another?" he asked.

Jax shrugged. "Ain't got nothin' better to do."

He shook his head. A soft frown ghosted across his lips long enough for Jax to notice before he shrugged. "Now you know how I feel about Donna."

As his brother walked over to the bar, Jax watched him, his arm sliding down Donna's backside as he approached her.

It was one thing to warm your bed with the first thing available in town, but Donna Draper was trouble. She had stirred a lot of shit for Sam last year. She had lied about her relationship with Blake and almost ruined Sam's and Blake's chance at happiness. For Jax, that qualified as a no-dick deal breaker.

However, he sensed Dylan was going through something right now, and there was a history between his little brother and the dumb blonde with the famous double D's. He only hoped Dylan would get his act together before he ended up with consequences he'd regret, like a damn baby or, for God's sake, herpes.

Just as Jax was contemplating the situation, his phone lit up on the table, and he saw a text from his dad. He hoped it wasn't a play-by-play of some dumbass encounter with a widowed hot mama that liked to play shuffleboard.

But as he read through the message, he realized it was much worse.

Dad

Expect a visit from a real estate analyst to-morrow

Dad

Old friend of the family

Dad

Her name is Allison Hanover

Dad

And be nice, Jax!

Who the hell was Allison Hanover?

Chapter Two

Allison

In a world full of men, be a woman.

The sticky note tucked into the corner of Allison Hanover's bedroom mirror served as a reminder that the world she lived in was far from easy. With its men in three-piece suits and six-figure salaries, she worked twice as hard as the male analysts, got half the recognition, and still made less money.

Despite this, she knew she was the best analyst at Ryder Investments, and she didn't need any validation from a red-blooded male to affirm that information for her.

Settling onto her bed, she closed her eyes and began her early morning girl power hour. Engulfed in the empowering lyrics of Taylor Swift's "The Man," she focused on her breathing exercises.

She sat cross-legged on her bed, staring out the large window of her apartment that overlooked downtown Erie.

She had chosen her apartment not only because of its proximity to her office but also for its placement high above the city. Looking down on unsuspecting people as they went about their day-to-day activities was something Allison did often. Somehow, it made her feel less lonely, less disconnected from the world. Climbing the corporate ladder meant making choices early in her career that weren't compatible with long-term friendships.

Being a woman wasn't easy for her. Back when she started out, she felt like she had to compromise the values she held most dear. Sometimes she didn't play fair, manipulating situations to edge out her peers and secure contracts at the firm. The ends justified the means, right?

When she achieved the position of senior consultant at her firm, she bought her first pair of real Louboutin high-heeled shoes. Strutting into the office the next day, she felt like a goddamn queen.

Her boss, Chip Ryder, assured her she wouldn't even remember the name of the guy whose account she had stolen to get the promotion. Surprisingly, he was right. She couldn't recall his name, yet the guilt she felt when she closed her eyes ... Well, that haunted her every single night, even though she would never mention that to Chip.

As she climbed off her bed, she made her way into the kitchen to prepare her morning breakfast. It was always a green kale smoothie and a banana, a routine she never skipped. Starting the day off right was important to Allison. Sipping her smoothie, she carried it back to her room and dressed for the day. She chose a black pencil skirt that accentuated her tall, slim frame, along with a black pinstripe jacket paired with a white dress shirt. And, of course, she completed the look with her black Louboutin heels. Allison believed a woman had every right to feel like she just stepped out of a magazine, especially before entering the lion's den of men who awaited her.

Her mother, a criminal defense attorney and senior partner at a prestigious Erie law firm, always told her, *"You were born an original. Don't be a copy."* Being the only female at Ryder Investments was about as original as she could get.

She had met her boss, Chip, at a bar near her apartment in downtown Erie, right out of college. He was charming, easy on the eyes, and quite persistent in his pursuit of her. Perhaps it was because she was drinking that night, something she did only on rare occasions, that she found it hard to resist his advances. Their relationship lasted briefly over the next few months, during which he was pleasant enough. The sex was good, though mostly one sided when it came to gratification. However, she knew deep down that the relationship was a lot like a gallon of milk—it would spoil quickly and need to be thrown out.

While her prediction about the relationship turned out to be true, fate had other plans. Once the relationship soured, Chip surprised her by offering her a job at his real estate firm. Initially, she had been resistant to accept the offer, fearing that it would appear that he had offered the job simply because of their past relationship. But after considering her options, she decided to take advantage of every opportunity given to her and prove to everyone at the firm that she was worthy of the job.

For the next year, Chip kept things strictly platonic, taking her under his wing to mentor her on the accounts she worked and praising each job she landed at the firm. He even encouraged her to make more "ruthless" moves that eventually catapulted her status amongst her peers.

Eventually, though, Chip crossed a line when she discovered him inventing excuses for them to work late together. His hands would wander when they were alone, touching her knee or offering to massage her shoulders after a late-night assignment. Falling back into his bed wasn't something she was proud of. Chip Ryder was a looming and intimidating presence.

She tucked a lock of her auburn hair behind her ear, pressing her lips together, their vibrant red hue perfectly stained. Gathering her keys and purse, she stepped out of her apartment and casually tapped the elevator button. While waiting, she glanced down at her phone to read the morning news, a part of her daily ritual to stay informed about current events. Some may call it doom scrolling, but she believed it was important to be educated about politics and world news.

She scanned the real estate hashtags for any news related to downtown sell offs or incoming businesses that might be important investments for the firm's future, just in case she needed to sniff around and get a head start on future clients.

The elevator bell chimed, signaling her arrival at the garage level, and she walked into the dimly lit area, gripping her keys tightly as she clicked the button on her fob. In the distance, she heard her sleek black Mazda MZ 5 Miata chirp. The car was a testament to everything she had accomplished the last few years. She could afford pretty much anything she needed at this point in her life. It felt good not to have to rely on her parents for anything anymore.

As she was about to reach her car, the phone in her hand began buzzing, causing her to pause. To her surprise, a name she hadn't heard from in a long time popped up on the screen: Ken Lancaster. He was a friend of her parents from her hometown of Titusville, Pennsylvania. Well, if she could even call it her hometown. Her parents had lived there until she was born, but she had only called it home until she was three months old. That was when her parents left town, and her dad accepted a job as the Chief of Medicine at UPMC Mercy Hospital.

Ken and his wife, Mary, had been friends with her parents back in high school. Unfortunately, Mary had passed away from cancer when Allison was just eight years old. It wasn't until last year that she had the chance to meet any of the Lancasters when Ken reached out to her about selling his auto shop. Chip had been very interested in the potential purchase. The shop was old but also the only one in the small town, which meant money in Chip's eyes. However, Ken had pulled back on the deal, much to Chip's complete displeasure, and instead sold the shop to his oldest son.

When she last spoke to Ken, Allison thought he seemed like a nice man—friendly, if not a bit abrasive—but genuinely interested in what was best for his business.

She answered the phone quickly. "Hey, Ken, it's Allison. How are you?"

His pleasant voice came through the line, and he seemed calmer compared to their last conversation. "Allison, so glad I caught you before work," he said.

"How can I help you today?" she asked, as she settled into the driver's seat of her car.

He chuckled. "Always right to the point, Allison. A woman after my own heart." After a brief pause, it was clear he had something on his mind. "Remember last year when I asked for help with my shop?"

"I do. I believe you ended up selling it to family, correct?" Uncertain of what this conversation was leading to, she wondered if his son had changed his mind about buying the shop.

"Yes, my son, Jackson." His voice remained calm, but she sensed a hint of apprehension in his words. "He's great at the work part, always was. But uh, the finance stuff isn't really his strong suit."

Puzzled, she couldn't understand why he was sharing this with her. After all, she wasn't an accountant. "That sounds like something we hear from a lot of business owners when we step in to purchase their business, sir."

He quickly interjected, "Please, my father was a sir. Ken is fine."

She provided him a friendly laugh before responding. "Of course, Ken. So, what exactly did you want me to do? Was he wanting to sell?"

"Heavens, no. Not at all." Now she was even more perplexed. She pushed the start button on her car, and it revved to life. "I was talking to your mom actually, and she suggested, well, we were thinking, maybe you could do me a favor and drive down there and help him figure it out."

"I'm sorry what?" The call switched to the car's speaker, and she thought she must have misheard him. Surely, he wasn't asking her to go to Titusville to teach his kid how to manage his finances.

"I'm not asking for a lot. He knows how to run the garage, and he's a smart kid but, he just needs help to understand what he's looking at," Ken pleaded desperately on the other end. He was a nice old man, and Allison hated to turn him down outright. Looking up at the green light ahead, she pulled into the garage at her office.

"Can I get back to you later today? This isn't exactly my area of expertise. My job is more about research and purchasing, but, of course, I would have to talk to my boss before I agreed to anything. I have a lot of clients on my plate right now," she said, sighing as she thought about her overflowing case load sitting on her desk.

"Sure can, dear. Just let me know," Ken said, his friendly voice already fueling the guilt swirling in her head. She knew that later that evening, she would politely turn down his offer, but first, she would need to come up with some excuse.

Because there was no way she was going to Titusville.

"Earth to Allie Cat!" Chip's voice snapped Allison out of her thoughts, and she looked up to see him staring at her from the head of the conference table. She couldn't stand it when he called her Allie Cat, especially when he did it in front of the rest of the team.

She realized she hadn't been paying attention since walking into the meeting and quickly tried to recover. "Sorry, we were talking about the Sanderson building, right?" She glanced at the presentation on the large screen behind her boss.

"Thanks for catching up," he said. The sarcastic tone immediately had her peers straightening in their seats, looking around the room and whispering to each other with snide grins.

Feeling a surge of frustration, she stood up and walked to the front of the room, elevating her voice as she spoke. "Well, after talking to George Riggs, who is the son of the owner, Ralph, I found out that his dad is having financial trouble. This is because of a failed investment last year in one of the waterfront buildings he was purchasing for a merger that fell through."

Her boss shook his head with a smile. "How did you get that information out of him?"

She shrugged, setting her shoulders back. "Mr. Riggs enjoys Brandy." Glancing back at the screen, she clicked to the next slide.

"The property is assessed at three-point-five million dollars. However, when I spoke to Mr. Riggs, he let it slip that his father had also been lax in their last safety inspection. And the building is facing several code violations. I believe we can get them to accept a much lower offer if we go in with that information."

Chip smirked. "I'm assuming the elder Mr. Riggs does not know that we are aware of this information?"

She nodded, maintaining her focus on the screen. "Of course not." Clicking again, she continued. "The only other firm going after the building is Axon, and George told me that his father and Stan Axon are old golfing buddies. So, if we want to make the deal, we need to move now."

One of the partners, sitting on the other end of the table, directed a venomous gaze at her. "What makes you think that Mr. Riggs won't sell to his old buddy Axon, anyway?"

She calmly placed the remote back on the table and walked back to her seat, licking her lips. "Because Ralph Riggs is sleeping with Mr. Axon's wife."

The man gasped; his eyes now fixed on Chip. "Is this the kind of information you sanctioned us to gather?"

Chip let out a whistle, clearly pleased with the turn of events. "This is the kind of intel that makes us winners, Larry." He turned off the projector and slapped the table with glee. "Now, get out there and do your jobs, losers." The men stared at each other for a moment, unsure of what to do, before finally standing and exiting the room, grumbling to each other.

As soon as she found herself alone with her boss, he let out another whistle. "Damn, good job, Allie Cat," he said.

She scowled, turning to face him with a venomous glare. "I told you not to call me that in front of people."

Playfully, he pursed his lips and glided toward her. "What's wrong with you today? You seem distracted. I was almost angry when you weren't paying attention."

She closed her eyes and exhaled. "Sorry, I just have to tell a nice old guy that I can't help him with something, and I'm not sure how to let him down."

He furrowed his brow, crossed his arms, and leaned against the table. "What nice old man? I've never known you to have a problem letting a man down." Allison glared at him. "Oh, come on Allie, I'm just kidding."

She looked down at her phone, clearly preoccupied. "You remember Ken Lancaster? The auto shop guy last year."

He perked up and leaned toward her. "The one who pulled out last minute, right? The Titusville place?"

She shook her head with a soft sigh. "Yeah, that one."

"Now wait a minute. Why are you turning him down?"

With her lips pressed tightly together, she glared. "Because I'm not a damn accountant. Why would I go help some hillbilly figure out math?"

"Math?"

Inhaling deeply, she leaned against the conference table. "His son, the one who ended up buying the place, is struggling. His dad wants me to drive to Titusville and help him figure out how to do his finances, like I'm a damn accountant. Can you believe that?" Chip's face lit up like he'd just won the lottery. "What?"

He stepped closer and ran his fingers through her hair. "Baby, don't you see the perfect opportunity that has just presented itself to us?"

Irritated, she slapped his hand away and sat back down in her chair. "I'm not following you, Chip."

"Go to Titusville, show the guy how hard it is to run his shop, then get him to sell it to you. It's brilliant." He shrugged and leaned over to kiss her forehead. "I want that shop, Allie Cat, and I want you to get it for me."

She stood up, shaking her head at him with her hands balled firmly at her side. "I'm not going to some small town to talk some guy out of his store. I'm already working the Sanderson Building. That's millions of dollars, Chip. That shop's gotta be worth only a few hundred thousand."

He waved his hand in front of her face, a gesture that irritated her. "I'll put Larry on the Sanderson job. I want the Titusville shop."

All her hard work, and yet he was just handing it over to Larry? She couldn't believe it. She wanted to protest, but it was clear from the look on his face that he'd already made up his mind. Resigned, she sighed. "Fine, I'll go to Titusville, but I'm not guaranteeing anything."

His response was infuriating. "Good girl!" he said, his palm touching her cheek. She closed her eyes, fighting back her anger. *Good girl!* As if she was some submissive chick just writhing in her panties, waiting for some domineering billionaire to tell her what to do.

She took a moment to collect herself, forcing a smile before opening her eyes. She stood and met his gaze. "I'll go home and pack a bag."

"Don't forget to check in with me and let me know your progress. Do whatever you gotta do to get an offer, Allie Cat," Chip said with a menacing grin. As she walked away, she winced at the sting of his hand on her backside. "See ya when you get back to town, and we'll celebrate, tiger," he called after her.

Feeling a mix of frustration and determination, she scowled as she walked out of the office. She pulled out her phone and quickly texted Ken Lancaster.

Allison

Let Jackson know I'll be there tomorrow

Chapter Three

Jackson

After speaking to his sister on the phone the previous evening, Jax was unable to solve the mystery of Allison Hanover. Surprisingly, Sam had never heard of her either, despite their father referring to her as an "old friend" of the family.

In an attempt to uncover more information, Jax searched the main house, coming across an old address book in the junk drawer of the kitchen. Though he found a listing for a Chuck and Stacy Hanover in Erie, there was no specific mention of an Allison.

Dylan seemed to think he was overreacting to the entire thing, which was hilarious coming from him, but his brother didn't have to take school lessons from some old fogey who would look down her nose at him like she was smarter than him, either.

Determined to ease his nerves, Jax brought along his dog Whiskey to work with him that morning. While it was uncommon for Whiskey to accompany him to the shop, he found that having his loyal companion by his side made dealing with troublesome people more bearable.

And he had already made up his mind that Allison Hanover simply sounded unbearable.

He was probably being irrational about that. Yeah, he was definitely being irrational. But he just didn't have time to worry about some city slicker that his dad was sending to come sniffing around his business. No matter how much the process for the finances confused him, he'd figure it out—eventually. He just needed the time to do it.

Stepping out of his office, he checked the chart to see what work was waiting for them. Dylan was already working on an oil change for Ron Chase's kid. There was an engine rebuild needing done in Bay 2, but that was waiting on a part that should be delivered sometime today. He tossed the clipboard to the counter and walked over to his unfinished project in the corner. It would be hours before he had to do any official work, so now was as good a time as any to work on his bike.

Popping a few aspirins into his mouth to deal with the annoying pain in his hip he so joyfully woke up with, he spun the knob clockwise on the radio, the music crackling loudly throughout the shop as Warrant's "Cherry Pie" echoed throughout the garage.

There were parts stacked precariously in the shop's corner and all over the floor, just as he had left them the last time he had worked on the bike. At the rate he had been going, he was never going to finish it.

The air in the garage was sweltering for a hot July day, and the small fan in the corner rafters wasn't getting the job done. Reaching down, he peeled off his shirt, tossing it to the floor as he bent down to pick up his wrench and a part to place on the bike. Sweat was already coating his skin, accumulating on his brow as it dripped to the ground beside him.

With a loud grunt, he twisted the wrench on a stuck bolt, swearing loudly and tossing it to the ground when the damn thing didn't move.

A loud clicking sound quickly diverted his attention. He looked over his shoulder and saw a pair of long, slender legs coming into view, accompanied by the click clack of black heels with each step. As his eyes scanned up her toned legs to her slim waist and firm hips, he was met with a pair of steel-blue eyes and copper red hair.

He had to inhale sharply to keep from swearing. This was the kind of woman that men went to war for.

She looked like she just walked off the pages of one of his porn magazines. With her fuck me heels and white button-up shirt, he wasn't sure if he should ask her for a blow job or beg her for mercy. The firm expression on her glossy red lips made her as lethal as a heart attack.

The sun reflected against her fire-streaked hair as she stood staring at him with her hands on her hips. She shined brighter than a lightning bug in June. Whiskey barked, jumping up from his spot in the corner and trotting over to his side. He noticed the woman flinch slightly. Jax leaned down and patted the pup's head. "You lost, Firefly?"

Her high-pitched voice was calm, yet elevated. "Excuse me?"

He tilted his head and glanced at Dylan, who was gawking at their newest arrival. "Can I help you with anything?" He tilted his head, shifting his gaze behind her, noticing the fancy sports car she arrived in. "Something broke on your wheels?"

She glanced toward the car and laughed. "Oh, no, I don't need any work done."

He looked her up and down. "That's a damn shame."

He could sense the moment her demeanor switched from confusion to a more professional and curt tone. "Are you Jackson Lancaster?"

He nodded. "I am, and who might you be?"

With a hint of annoyance, she straightened her back. "Allison Hanover. I believe your father told you to expect me."

Well, hell, that was the quickest way to get rid of a boner.

Dylan snorted across the room, and he shot him a dirty look. Jax stood up, wiped his greasy hands against his jeans, and walked toward her, extending his hand. "So, you're the suit," Jax said. "My apologies for not having our red carpet washed and ready this morning."

She stared down at his hand, her nose crinkling momentarily, before simply nodding. "Mr. Lancaster, your father, mentioned you didn't understand how to run your finances, and he needed me to teach you."

He yanked his hand back to his side, staring at her before taking a deep breath. "It sounds like you've been misinformed, sweetheart. My father means well, but all of this is really unnecessary."

She laughed, but it wasn't a polite laugh. It was one of those sounds one made that implied they were better than him, and he didn't appreciate it. "I see," she said, her lips turning upward as she looked around the garage before speaking again. "So, I'm sure that your balance sheets are all updated." He nodded as if he understood her and agreed. "I know last year when I reviewed your P&L, your dad was really focused on reducing your operating expenses to increase your gross profit, and I'm sure you've looked at your COGS."

Jax blinked at her, unsure of how to reply. Of course, this was when Dylan chose the moment to speak. "Jax is all about our COGS," he said, nodding at Jax with a proud grin.

"Shut the fuck up, Dyl." He glared at his brother, turning back toward the fiery redhead. "My L&P is all in line last time I reviewed it, and we have all our expenses paid for," he confidently declared, looking back at Dylan and winking.

She rolled her eyes. "Wow, your dad wasn't kidding."

"What the hell is that supposed to mean?" he said in a low growl.

Her nonchalant shrug as she clacked across the concrete floor pissed him off even more. "He just said you had no idea how to do any of this."

Well, gee thanks for the vote of confidence Dad!

"Yeah, well, as you can see from all the cars in here, we're doing just fine," he said with every ounce of pride he could muster.

"For how long, Mr. Lancaster?" She turned toward him, her blue eyes staring through him. "It's one thing to get your hands dirty. It's another thing entirely to be able to maintain it."

He stepped closer toward her, smirking when he noticed her flinch as he got within touching distance. "Sweetheart, I think you'll find I got no problem maintaining."

She held his gaze, not backing down, and dammit if he didn't like a challenge. "You'll be out of business in three months." As she spoke, her eyes never left his, and he felt the anger boil inside of him. He was not going to let this city girl come in here and tell him he was going to fail at what he'd worked his entire life for. He might not be familiar with all the fancy acronyms she was tossing around, but he wasn't a damn idiot.

"Get out," he said loudly, flexing his fingers at his side.

Startled, she blinked. "Excuse me?"

He leaned against his counter, glaring at her. "Are you deaf? I said, get out. Do I need to say it in a different language for you city folk? I don't need your help, nor do I want it."

"You're a damn fool," she said. "You won't last the year without understanding operating expenses, gross profit, or cost of goods." Her face softened. "Your dad isn't joking, Mr. Lancaster. You need my help."

"Yeah, well, my dad is wrong," he said, his jaw tightening. "We're fine. Go back to the city, Firefly. I've survived my whole life without needing help from a city slicker. I'll be damned if I let one in the door now." She began to open her mouth to argue, but he hollered, "I said get out!"

Startled, she jumped. "You are—impossible. And—rude," she screeched.

He pinched his lips together, clenching his jaw. "Harsh words, did your mother teach you those?"

She turned and stormed out of the garage, the click of her heels on the concrete echoing through the space. Her skirt hugged her tightly, swishing with the force of her anger. It was a shame they had met the way they had. If it had been under any other circumstance, he would have done things to that woman's body she would have remembered for years.

She stopped abruptly by the trunk of her car, a high-pitched groan emitting from her throat as she kicked furiously at the ground. He watched as she tried to pull her pretty black heel out of the dirt, her foot coming free from the shoe. She angrily yanked it from the ground and limped the rest of the way to her car before slamming the door behind her and squealing her tires out of the driveway.

A damn shame indeed!

Chapter Four

Allison

"What an insufferable, pompous, obstinate—" she growled in frustration as her foot pressed down on the pedal of her accelerator. Jackson Lancaster was about the most irritating man she had ever met. He obviously had no clue what he was talking about when it came to running a business. "L&P," she grumbled with a snort. "What a moron."

There was no way she would be offering any kind of assistance to that dolt of a man-child. Not to mention the nerve he had staring at her with those blue eyes, or that strong, stubbled jaw clenched tightly on his irritatingly handsome face. The absolute gall he had to ogle her body like she was some sort of cracker jack prize. She was a senior partner with a six-figure salary, for God's sake!

Punching Ken Lancaster's phone number onto the screen on her dash, she waited as the phone connected. "Allison, so happy to hear from you. How did it go with Jax?" he asked cheerily.

She groaned, "I'm sorry, but I just don't think I can help your son." She kept her voice firm but decisive, leaving him no room to change her mind.

"Did something happen? I know that Jax can be a bit—"

She cut him off. "Abrasive? Rude? Completely inappropriate?" She offered him some suggestions, hoping he got her point.

"Well, apparently you caught him on a good day." He chuckled, but she clearly was in no mood for joking as she turned onto the main road heading out of town with a squeal of her tires.

"He doesn't want my help, and I think it's for the best that I don't give it to him," she said.

He sighed into the phone. "Look, I know my son can be rough around the edges." She snorted, but he continued speaking anyway. "Jax lost his mother when he was very young. I raised that boy the best I could." She blinked. She did not want to feel any empathy for the man she just left standing back at that shop. "He loves that place more than anything in this world, well, except maybe for his dog. Perhaps sending you in there the way I did was the wrong approach."

"Sending me in there at all was the wrong approach," she said, staring up at the stoplight impatiently waiting for it to change. "He doesn't want help."

"That's where you're wrong," he said. "He's just too stubborn to ask for help."

"Ken, there is stubborn and then there is whatever your son is," she said.

"Can you just give him another chance, Allison? I know he can be tough to deal with, but I promise you, he needs you." He sounded so sincere and honestly desperate that Allison felt her defenses crumbling.

She had never been needed by anyone in her life before.

"I don't know, Ken."

The apprehension in her voice must have been loud, because it was almost like Ken could sense her defenses failing. "Perhaps let him think it's his idea. Jax does better when people don't tell him what to do."

Without thinking, she snorted. "Problem with authority?"

"Something like that," Ken said. "Just guide him into it gently, and I think you'll get more out of him."

She thought about her approach at the garage today and perhaps Ken may have a point. She may have come on too strong. While it was true that she thought Jackson would be out of business in three months without her help, there might have been a more effective way to convey that. And it was possible that calling him a damn fool might have been a step out of line in trying to get him on her side. He was just so infuriating.

"Fine. I'll try again tomorrow," she said, sighing in resignation.

"Thanks, Allison." The happiness in his voice shouldn't have made her feel so good. "There's a bed-and-breakfast in town off Main Street called Hattie's. Tell Mrs. Hattie that Ken sent you. She'll take good care of you."

The call ended, leaving her alone with her thoughts as she turned around at the next stop sign. She had to accept that she was stuck in Titusville another day and that she was going to have to face off with Jackson Lancaster once more.

The two-story home was on a small grassy hill and seemed pleasant enough to spend the night. Allison parked her car on the side of the road and gathered her things. Looking up at the sign on the side of the home that Ken had sent her to, identified it as Hattie's Bed and Breakfast, a historic site registered with the state of Pennsylvania.

She entered the house through a pair of large red doors. The inside of the bed-and-breakfast was not at all what she was used to in her modern apartment back home. The patterns on the wall were floral and busy. A mixture of pinks and mauves swirled in an array of flowers on a velvet wallpaper. She was sure it was quaint for a sweet old grandmother, but not exactly her style.

Allison wandered through the spacious living room, glancing at the books strewn about the built-in bookshelves. Suddenly, an elderly voice interrupted her thoughts, causing her to jump. "Most of those belonged to my mother," the voice said.

"I didn't mean to intrude, I um..." Feeling uncomfortable, she walked away from the bookshelf and shuffled herself back into the small hallway. "I needed a room. Ken Lancaster told me this was the place to stay," she said.

The woman's stern face melted into a warm smile. "Ah, Kenny, always looking out for me. I miss that handsome devil around here." The woman walked toward a small desk in the hall. She picked up a book and opened it to a page that was nearly empty of entries. She wondered how the woman stayed in business. "How long will you be staying, dear?"

Allison quickly responded, "Oh, just the night."

"What brings you to town?" She shuffled around in the desk drawer for a pen.

Allison teased her lip with her teeth before replying. "I'm just doing Ken a favor with his son."

The woman's sly smile spread on her face. "Which one would that be, dear? He has two."

Taking the pen from the woman, Allison wrote her name on the line she directed her to. "Oh, um, I'm helping Jackson with some financial things for his shop."

"Such a sweet boy that Jackson." She glanced up at her quickly, unsure if the woman was deaf or had just not heard her correctly.

"No, Jackson Lancaster, the oldest one."

"Oh yes, Jax, tall and scruffy, like a sexy Paul Bunyan," she said with a little growl, as she glanced down at the name she had written on the register. "I'll tell you, Allison, if I was your age, I'd climb that boy like a tree."

"Oh!" Allison reacted with surprise.

"Don't look at me like that. I still have eyes," the woman said, waving her off. She then reached up to grab a key from the board and handed it to Allison.

"I'm not saying he isn't easy on the eyes, ma'am," Allison said with a laugh. "Perhaps just a little difficult to get along with."

The silver-haired woman responded with a wink, "You attract more bees with honey than vinegar." She climbed the stairs, leaving Allison standing at the bottom, still dumbfounded by the conversation. "Are you coming, dear?" she asked, staring down at her.

Allison looked up at the red-carpeted staircase, blinking. "Um, yeah, right behind you."

Mrs. Hattie had advised her that there was no Thai food in town, which was disappointing to hear. Thai food had always been her go to comfort food in the city, something she had readily available on the ground floor of her apartment building. Not having the familiarity of her everyday routine available to her, she had asked the woman for something in town she could try instead.

The woman swore by this little diner at the other end of Main Street. She opted to walk the three blocks and get in some exercise for the evening. She was thankful she had waited until after her shower to eat dinner. The sweltering heat had dissipated with the setting sun. The town streets were not like the busy city blocks back home. Titusville lacked the congestion of cars bustling back and forth. Instead, there were neighbors sitting on porches, kids on bikes riding through the streets, and friendly faces happy to wave hello as she walked by.

She always wondered if it was awful, living where everyone knew your name and what you ate for dinner. Back home, the only person who really knew who she was at her apartment was her doorman, Jim. Her neighbors mostly kept to themselves. She'd only seen them once or twice and didn't have a clue what any of them did for a living. The only reason she knew the name of the woman who lived across the hall was because she accidentally got her mail once. It might seem like a lonely existence, but it worked for her.

As she turned the corner, her phone buzzed in her pocket. She answered it to hear Chip's voice on the other end. "Allie Cat, tell me good news."

She should have known he would have expected her to have already arrived and achieved the task he set out for her. "I've only been here for a few hours. And I told you not to get your hopes up, Chip."

She could feel his irritation radiate through the phone. "How hard can it be to convince some small town nobody to sell me his shop? Surely you didn't show up there and find a math genius that understood his gross profit margin already?"

"No, Chip, I'm not sure what he knows honestly," she replied, her voice wavering. "But I already warned you that this guy doesn't want to sell."

He chuckled, and she switched the phone to her other ear, not wanting to hear his voice any longer. "Fine, so what are you planning to do to get him to sell to me?" he asked.

"I'm staying the night. I'll plan to go back over there in the morning." She sighed in frustration. She wasn't interested at all in getting Jackson to sell his shop to Ryder Investments. "But Chip, you have to be willing to concede that this might never happen."

"Don't disappoint me. You know I hate that," he said before hanging up the phone, ending the call before she could even say goodbye. He had a habit of doing that. Something that always left her feeling unimportant.

Hanging her head, she pocketed her phone and looked up. She was standing outside the diner, her chest moving slowly as she breathed in a shaky breath. The bright neon sign read "Linda's Diner" and glowed against the night sky. She hoped they had something healthy for her to eat.

Stepping into the noisy diner, a friendly woman greeted her. "Welcome to Linda's. Sit anywhere you want. I'll be right over."

Looking around, she found the place packed. Apparently, this was the place to be on a Friday night.

She found a cozy seat in a corner booth, sliding all the way to the window to hide away from the rest of the diners. A chirpy woman about her age, with brown skin and dark hair, bounced toward her with a menu and slid it across the table. "Hey, I'm Jamila. I'm pretty new here, but I've never seen you around before."

"Yeah, I'm only here for the night," she said. Glancing at the menu, she found exactly what she expected from a diner—a lot of oil and burgers. "You got anything healthy, like a salad?"

The girl snorted and stared back at her, expressionless. "Oh, you're serious?"

"Yeah." She nodded. *How did this place not have a salad?*

"Uh, let me go ask Linda." The woman walked away, heading toward what appeared to be an office. Meanwhile, Allison stared down at her phone, scrolling through her latest news feeds to catch up on the day's information.

"Hi, I'm Linda." The newest woman, older yet even friendlier than the previous waitress, introduced herself. "Jamila says you were looking for something that's not on the menu."

"A salad," she said, frowning. "Sorry, I didn't realize it would be trouble."

"Oh dear, no, that's no trouble," Linda assured her. She then turned to Jamila. "Maybe we can see if Jason can make one out of the burger ingredients."

"You really don't have to do that," Allison argued, only to be waved off by Linda.

"Really, it's no problem at all. Sorry, I didn't catch your name?" Linda asked.

"It's Allison." She smiled. "I really appreciate you doing this. I'm only visiting for the night, so I promise not to make this a regular issue."

"Oh, a newbie, we don't get a ton of visitors who stay the night," Linda said. "Do you mind if I ask what brings you to our tiny town?"

This caught Allison off guard. Though it really shouldn't have. Small towns really were in everyone's business. She exhaled with a light chuckle. "Um, just doing a favor for a friend of the family, Mr. Lancaster."

The woman's face lit up like a Roman candle. "Well, then that makes you a friend of my family, as well," she continued. "The Lancasters are practically related to the Forresters. Well, I suppose I'm getting ahead of myself, but a mother can hope, can't she?" Allison must have had the most confused look on her face because the woman immediately clarified. "Sorry, my son Blake, and Ken's daughter, Sam, live together in New York, and I keep hoping for those two lovebirds to get hitched, eventually."

Linda must have sensed Allison's overwhelm and unease because she turned back to Jamila, who had returned to the table. "Did we get the salad ordered?"

The waitress nodded. "All done, Mrs. F."

"Wonderful, well, you just let me know if you need anything else, Allison," Linda replied before excusing herself back to the office behind the counter.

With a laugh, Jamila whispered, "She's really nice, but she can be a lot to take in if you aren't from around here. I've only been here for four months, and I'm still getting used to it."

Allison smiled. "It was a lot of information to download in a short amount of time."

The waitress nodded. "Let me know if you need anything else."
Allison watched her walk away and stared out the window of the
diner at the empty streets outside.

It was nothing like downtown Erie; small towns were so different from where she grew up. She wasn't sure she could get used to
knowing everyone's business. Sure, Mrs. Hattie, Jamila, and Linda
seemed like genuinely nice people, but Allison was a shark, and
sharks didn't belong in fish tanks.

Chapter Five

Jackson

Jax woke up on Saturday morning with a dull ache in his leg, which made him particularly grouchy this morning. His sister's text greeted him the moment he opened his eyes, something that usually brought him a bit of joy to his day.

Sam

So? Is the mystery of Allison solved?

He stared at the phone, grimacing, unsure of how to reply.

Yup, she was a pain in my ass!

She was sex in 5-inch heels that turned out to be the devil in disguise!

Instead, he opted for the simple truth.

Jax

Dads idea of a twisted joke

Jax

I took care of her. Sent her packing back to the city

Sam

Glad you got that figured out then

Sam

Miss you loser

Jax

Miss ya too sis

With a smile on his face, and the morning family texting session complete. He figured the grouchiness would soon subside, but clearly, life had other ideas for his day.

The ache in his body was still conspiring against him. Unfortunately, that wasn't the end of his misery. As he rushed to get ready for work, he faced a series of unfortunate events. First, his bread burned in the toaster. Second, his dog Whiskey refused to leave his comfortable bed when he tried to let him out. And finally, his old truck refused to start.

Jax spent an annoying amount of time tinkering around with the engine, jiggling the belt, muttering a few curse words, and even offering an ultimatum to the dear Lord. The truck sputtered to life just as Dylan wandered out of the house disheveled and yawning, completely oblivious that Jax had been outside for the last twenty minutes, sweating profusely.

He only hoped this wasn't an omen for the rest of his day. However, as he pulled up to the garage, it became clear that hope was out of the question.

Leaning against the doorframe of the shop, Allison Hanover looked out of place and completely disinterested. Her clothing, while definitely not unpleasant, was once again inappropriate for the hot and greasy garage. She was wearing a dark skirt that clung to the curve of her hips, a tight flowered button-up shirt and, once again, ridiculously high heels that had no business being worn in the dirt and soil of any garage.

Engrossed in scrolling on her phone, she barely glanced up as he pulled the truck into the grassy spot beside the building.

"I guess you didn't scare her off after all." Dylan chuckled beside him.

"Suppose I'll have to try harder." Stepping out of the truck with a grumble, he bit back the pain as he tried to overcompensate for his limp while walking toward her. "You lost? The city is back the other way."

"Sign says you opened an hour ago. Businesses lose revenue when the owners can't be responsible," she said, straightening up and dropping her phone into her purse. The shiny bag looked to be more expensive than half the clothes he owned.

"Thanks for the business tip," he said, pushing past her and shoving his key into the shop's door. "How much do I owe you?" With a forceful push, he swung the door open. Catching the roll of her eyes, he grumbled to himself as she followed him into the dark garage. "Why are you still here, Firefly?" he asked.

She was quick to correct him. "My name is Allison. And I told your father I would help you, and I intend to do that."

"Well, ain't you just the picture of good intentions?" The sarcasm in his voice dripped from his lips as her smile slipped from her face. "Alright, Firefly—" Emphasizing his nickname for her once again, stalking toward her, he hovered over her in the darkened garage.

Somewhere in the garage, his brother clicked on the lights, and they hummed softly on the other side of the room in one of the bays. While he could barely see her face, he could feel her body as she backed away from him, stumbling into a counter. Undeterred, he advanced toward her once more. He could hear a soft noise escape her dark red lips.

"You want to help me?" he growled. "I got a lot of ideas about how you could help me."

"Now you listen here—" she said, shifting on her feet.

He chuckled in response. "You really hate it when you aren't in charge, don't you?" Leaning over, he let his lips graze her ear as he whispered, "Must really piss you off that some low life townie isn't falling to his knees when you open your mouth."

She scoffed and shoved him backward, and he stumbled, trying to catch his step. The lights suddenly buzzed to life above their heads, and her bright blue eyes shone in irritation. "You are a spoiled asshole. Do you know that?"

He grinned maniacally, quite pleased with himself. "You got that the other way around, sweetheart. Besides, I think my mom would be proud. She really hated when us bottom feeders ended up as food for the blood-sucking corporate swindlers."

"Based on what I know of your mother, she'd be embarrassed to know her son was behaving like a neanderthal." Her eyebrow lifted with purpose as she glared at him. She must have known that she struck a nerve from the look on his face, because he swore she stumbled slightly on her feet before he spoke.

"Don't you dare speak about my mother," he growled, his shoulders squaring back. Breaking eye contact, he stalked through the garage, leaving her standing at the counter.

He ripped his shirt over his head, tossing it to the ground and dug out his tools. He sat down beside a Ford F150 parked in the bay. Lying back on the creeper, he rolled underneath the truck, breathing heavily as he tried to reel in his temper. "Get me that wrench, *Allison*." His voice sounded heavier than he intended.

The click-clack of heels resonated through the garage, ending with her tiny ankles standing just outside his view. "I'm sorry, what?" she asked.

"The wrench. Can you get it for me?" he repeated, a smirk playing on his lips. "It should be on the toolbox next to the truck."

"Can't you just get it yourself?" Her irritation caused her voice to squeak, and he almost wished he could see the pout on her pretty face. He couldn't deny that he enjoyed riling her up; she might be annoying as hell, but she was undeniably attractive when she was angry and flustered.

"It would be a lot easier if you got it for me," he said, his tone dripping with a sickening politeness. She clicked away from him, moving toward the toolbox. He watched her pretty ankles standing in front of it and heard the clanging sound of tools being moved about. The sound of her shoes alerted him to her return, and then she exhaled loudly as she forcefully shoved a tool against his leg, smacking him hard in the thigh. "Easy now," he warned, relieved it wasn't his bad leg.

Reaching blindly for the tool, he chuckled when his hand grasped the long, skinny screwdriver. Shoving himself out from under the truck, he looked up, only to catch a fleeting glimpse of white lace under her skirt.

Shit!

He quickly averted his eyes. He may be an asshole, but he wasn't *that* kind of asshole. "This is what you think a wrench looks like?" he teased, sending her a playful grin as she frowned down at him.

"Do I look like I work in a garage?" she shot back, her eyes blinking rapidly.

Lifting his chin, he gestured toward the tool he wanted. "See the one with the grip on the end of it?" She turned back and stomped toward the toolbox.

"This?" she asked, holding up a pair of needle-nose pliers. He shook his head. Suddenly, Dylan stalked over and handed her the wrench, not speaking as he walked away. "You could have just told me it was the silver one," she said with a pout, slapping it into his hand.

"And ruin all the fun? Not a chance," he said, rolling back under the truck. He tightened the bolt and glanced back to see her still standing outside the truck, behind his legs. Tinkering slowly underneath the truck, he completed his work and laid the wrench against his chest, staring at the underside of the truck. "So, uh, Allison, you said you were willing to help me out, right?" he asked.

"That's what I'm here for," she said with a groan, making him laugh as he shoved himself out from under the truck. She jumped away from him. He sat up on the creeper, patting his hands against his knees.

"Alright, sure then." Standing up, he crossed the garage, winking at Dylan as he watched him cautiously from the front of an old Chevy Blazer. Clicking on the radio, he grinned as the familiar voice of Bon Jovi filled the garage.

Her voice rose as she complained, "How are we supposed to hear each other over the music?"

The smirk on his lips grew wider as he turned away from his office, grabbing the clipboard from the wall of today's jobs ready to be completed. "I work better when there is background noise."

"Work? No, I'm not here to work, Mr. Lancaster," she said. Crossing her arms against her chest, she delighted him with her display of frustration. However, her gesture unintentionally caused her shirt to strain and the buttons to pry apart slightly. He should have looked away but stared, anyway. After all, he might not be a pervert, but he was still a hot-blooded man.

Grimacing in annoyance, he glared at her. "Jackson or Jax will be fine. Mr. Lancaster feels so ... unsatisfying, falling from those pretty lips."

"Fine!" she said, and he could feel the anger radiating from her. He shouldn't have taken so much joy in it, but hell, he did. "After all, I am here to help you, *Jackson*."

"That helped immensely," he said, raising an eyebrow playfully at the way his name fell from her mouth. "However, in case you didn't notice, you were already helping. In fact, I couldn't have finished that last job without that wrench." Licking his lips, he smirked, shaking the wrench in front of her face.

"Wrench?" she stuttered, clearly surprised. "No—I'm not..." Her pouty lips opened and closed as she struggled to find the right words. "I'm talking about the finances, Jackson."

His name really did sound pretty sweet coming from those lips, he thought, quickly dismissing it.

"Yeah, exactly. That's what you're helping me with. My finances. If I don't get these jobs done, well—I'm not going to make any money today, and that's gotta be bad for my revenue," he said, shrugging and stepping toward the next car in line. "Isn't that how you corporate fat cats put it?"

"Jackson," she squinted, "I'm a real estate analyst, not some grease monkey."

The slur caused him to turn sharply toward her. "Grease monkey? Is that what you really think of us?" He gestured toward his brother, then narrowed his eyes at her. "Well, Princess, us low lives may be beneath your feet, but this is our livelihood we're talking about."

She groaned in frustration. It was clear she was tiring of him and the situation. "That's not what I meant."

Sensing his advantage, he knew he had the upper hand. "Oh, I think you've made yourself perfectly clear about what you meant. Wouldn't you agree, Dylan?"

He looked at his brother, who seemed surprised and annoyed at being brought into the conversation. Shaking his head, he raised his hands. "Leave me out of whatever this is." He swiftly retreated from the garage, and Jax couldn't help but feel betrayed.

Traitor!

"You're clearly projecting your own biases onto things I didn't mean," she said, chin raised defiantly. Jax shrugged dismissively, knowing that he held the power in this situation. "I'm only here to help you with your books."

"Then leave," he said, turning away from her and approaching the Nissan that needed an oil change. "I have a lot of work to do this morning, and if I don't do it, no one else will." He stepped down, and his leg picked that moment to betray him. Stumbling, he desperately reached for the hood of the car to steady himself.

Allison rushed forward and grabbed his bare shoulder, and he swore his entire body shuddered. "Are you alright?" she asked, her voice filled with worry, her blue eyes staring into his.

"I'm fine," he growled, gripping the car to regain his composure. He wouldn't let his leg make him appear weak. Nodding, he reassured her again, "I'm fine."

As their eyes met once more, she cautiously assessed him. "I suppose I could spare an hour to assist you, at least until your brother returns," she mumbled.

"I don't need your pity, sweetheart," he snapped, limping over to the counter to grab his gloves. He shoved one glove onto his fingers with more force than necessary. Moving carefully toward the toolbox, he rummaged through it for his ratchet and torque wrench.

The last thing he needed was Allison Hanover's pity. Jackson wasn't an invalid. This woman already thought he was an idiot. He refused to let her see him as weak. Not that her opinion mattered at all. He didn't care what she thought about him. But the way she was looking at him now, he'd seen that look before. When he woke up in the hospital last year and everyone told him it was going to take months for him to walk again. Sure, Sam and Dylan supported him and pushed him in his recovery, but he saw the look in their eyes, the fear, the sadness for poor Ole Jax.

Well, to hell with that! He had never needed anyone's sympathy before—and he damn sure wasn't asking for it now. When the doc said it would take six weeks for him to walk again, he did it in four. Pity was for the weak and Jax's mama didn't raise no weak ass bitch.

Focusing on his task, he ignored the woman's gaze as he reached back for a clean rag, fumbling to find it without taking his eyes off the vehicle in front of him. It was only when his fingers brushed against flesh that he looked up, meeting her eyes as she handed him the rag. He grunted his thanks and then went to work on the task at hand in silence.

Chapter Six

Allison

Any form of empathy that Allison felt for Jackson's injury had worn off by the third hour of doing his "dirty work" around the garage. She had gathered tools with names she couldn't even pronounce, cleaned the counters, carried buckets of oil to dump into large bins, and even gotten him coffee. She had not fetched coffee for anyone since she was an intern!

The worst part of the entire day was that they hadn't talked about his books at all. After every vehicle, he would promise they would discuss it when he finished the next job, but there was always another job. Allison could see through his antics—she knew men like Jackson Lancaster. Egotistical, petty, so wrapped up in proving his point that he would fail at his own business just to watch her lose.

She growled as the last batch of oil spilled down the front of her skirt, dribbling onto the shop floor and down her legs. "Don't go getting that onto the concrete. Oil is a real bitch to clean up," she heard him say. She looked at her outfit, wanting to scream. To hell with the concrete floor. But she refused to let him see her angry.

Instead, she turned and smiled. "Won't happen again, boss," she said. She kept her tone professional, but stomped away from the oil drum and returned to the front of the car before she said anything she would regret.

The moment she got to the hood of the car, she heard a snap, her foot coming down harder than expected. She stumbled forward, grabbing onto the car for support, and a pair of muscular arms caught her around the waist. "Woah there, Firefly," he said. Turning in his arms, she looked up to find a pair of swirling blue eyes and a cocky smirk directed at her. "Can't have you getting hurt on my watch. I don't exactly understand my insurance coverage."

Swallowing hard, her body seemed to melt into the grip he had on her. Noting the way his biceps felt firm in her grasp, her eyes betrayed her as they slipped along the veins in his arms all the way up to his neck, where sweat was dripping down to his chest from the sweltering heat of the garage. "You alright there, Allison?" he asked.

Blinking, she snapped out of her daze, pulling away from him and staring down at her feet. "Dammit!" The crushing realization of what had happened hit her as she noticed her heel had split on the concrete.

"You need me to buy you a new pair of shoes up at the Dollar General?" he asked with a snicker, provoking her annoyance.

"Do you even know how much a pair of these cost?" she said, rubbing her forehead with her palm. She kicked off the shoe and hobbled to the counter to examine it. "I paid twenty-five hundred dollars for these."

"Are you shitting me?" she dismissed, refusing to acknowledge his presence. "Why were you even wearing those in the garage? They belong in a goddamn museum." He looked at her with his mouth draped open.

"Because I'm here to work on your damn finances, not doing manual labor, Jackson!" she whined slightly, grasping the shoe by the thread that was barely holding it together. There was no saving it.

"Yeah, well, maybe someone should talk to you about your own finances," he said, turning back toward the car he was working on. "I've never even thought about spending a hundred dollars on a pair of shoes, much less twenty-five hundred. Sounds like a ridiculous waste of money, if you ask me."

She pinched her eyes shut. Allison realized she was wasting her time and energy today. With all the dignity she could muster, she hobbled over to the counter and grabbed her purse, draping it over her shoulder. Inhaling deeply, she turned to face the man who had wasted her entire day. "I'm leaving," she said. The waver in her voice was an uncontrollable response.

As expected, he feigned shock. "Well now, don't leave on my account. It's been such a pleasure having you here in Titusville." The drip of sarcasm in his voice told her otherwise.

Stepping past him, she hurried to her car, navigating as best as a woman could in only one five-inch heel. "Don't you worry, Jackson Lancaster, I'll be back tomorrow," she said. She could have sworn she heard a soft curse behind her, which gave her great pleasure as she got into her car and drove away.

Allison walked up the stairs of the Bed and breakfast. She carried her shoes in her hand, happy to be alone again. However, she couldn't help but feel somewhat defeated after her day at the garage. Her skirt felt stiff, and the oil still clung to her legs from the multitude of times it had dripped onto her skin. All she wanted was to sink down into a hot bubble bath and cry.

"Oh, my!" a concerned voice sounded from below, interrupting her thoughts. Allison turned toward the woman and grimaced. "Child, you look terrible."

"It's been a really long day, Mrs. Hattie. I just want to take a hot bath and forget it even existed," Allison said, accompanied by a loud and miserable moan. She didn't honestly care about how pathetic she sounded. She turned her back and trudged the rest of the way up the stairs to her room. With frustration, she slammed the door closed behind her, trying to hold herself together. She really didn't need to turn into a blubbering mess tonight.

All she could think about was getting even. Peeling off each layer of sticky clothing from her skin, she felt more determined than ever. Tomorrow, she would waltz into that garage, demand to show that infuriating man what she had come to teach him and then get the hell out of Titusville forever. Jackson Lancaster would not defeat her.

She had known men like Jackson her whole life. Men took one look at her and made assumptions. Allison knew she was pretty. It wasn't arrogance. Her mother had raised her to appreciate the gifts she had given her at birth. She worked hard to keep her body in good shape. She went to the gym, ate healthy food, took care of her skin, and dressed in a way that accentuated her curves.

She learned early on that the only way to get what she wanted in life was to make it happen. No one was going to just give you what you wanted. She supposed she had her father to thank for that. Not that her parents weren't loving and kind, but she would use the term "museum parents" to best describe them. They weren't exactly affectionate. Hugging just wasn't something that was done when she was a child, so Allison stopped looking for that type of attention. Her parents gave her advice and support, but the expectation was that if she wanted something, she did it on her own. Just the way they had when they were young.

Men took one look at Allison and immediately labeled her a bitch. If she had been born a man, she would be called a "go-getter." *Double standards sucked!*

Once Allison had escaped to the privacy of the bathroom, she sank into the steaming water. She slid her headphones into her ears and turned up the volume on Halsey's "Nightmare" as it began playing. Closing her eyes, she rested her head against the back of the tub, hoping to let go the stress of the day.

The phone cut in, interrupting her music therapy, causing her to groan. However, when she saw it was Chip calling, she hesitated before touching the screen. Dealing with Chip Ryder was the last thing she wanted at this moment. Choosing to decline his call, she closed her eyes and smiled contentedly. Prioritizing herself felt damn good.

Chip Ryder could wait.

Allison bounced down the stairs after her bath, feeling lighter and much more optimistic than she had previously. By this time tomorrow, she would be returning to Erie, and everything would be back to normal.

She despised feeling out of place and disjointed. Ever since she had arrived in Titusville, that's exactly how she had felt. All she wanted was to go home and feel like herself again.

The moment she reached the bottom of the stairs, she spotted Mrs. Hattie sitting in her rocking chair, busy with her crochet. Cautiously, Allison approached her. "Hey, I wanted to apologize for earlier. I wasn't exactly friendly."

Setting her yarn on her lap, Mrs. Hattie looked up with a smile. "Oh dear, you're fine. It seems like you had quite the day."

Her sigh, as she settled into the chair beside her, wasn't intended to be that loud, but it felt intensely gloomy. "I'm not getting anywhere with Jackson," she said. "He simply will not listen to me."

"I assume the honey did not work?" The woman's soft smile was sweet, but not exactly helpful, either.

Allison shook her head, frustrated. "I worked at his garage all day today, broke my heel, ruined my skirt. He is maddening." Her jaw tightened when she spoke.

"I suppose there is a bit of madness in the boy's behavior when he's being stubborn," Mrs. Hattie acknowledged.

"Stubborn? No, Mrs. Hattie. This is more than that. I've never met anyone so bull-headed," Allison growled in frustration.

"Ah yes, a charmer he is indeed." She grinned, trying to hide her amusement.

Allison scoffed. "Charming? That man wouldn't know how to charm a woman if he fell on his head." She shook her head in exasperation. "He's completely impossible to have a conversation with. He's rude and barely calls me by my name like a normal human being."

The old woman giggled as if she was thirty years younger. "He must really like you."

Allison couldn't help but think how ridiculous that statement was. "He most certainly does not. I'm almost positive he hates my guts."

Mrs. Hattie simply shrugged. "So, what is your plan now?"

She squared her shoulders and pushed her shirt sleeves up her arms. "I'm giving him one more chance. After tomorrow, I'm going home. I will not waste another second on Jackson Lancaster!"

"Famous last words, dear." With a mischievous wink, the woman stood, placing her yarn into the basket beside her chair. "Have I ever told you the story of how I met Mr. Hattie?"

Allison narrowed her eyes at the elderly woman and sighed. "No, you have not, but I have a feeling you are about to."

"When I was nineteen, I came to Titusville as a young girl, wanting to find my way as a nurse. Honestly, I wasn't looking for love or a relationship. It wasn't easy having a career as a woman back then, either."

Allison empathized with her. The challenges women faced seemed like a never-ending story. "My John, he was a doctor here at the hospital. So handsome, yet so cocky." Mrs. Hattie chuckled.

"Aren't they all?"

Mrs. Hattie nodded. "Oh, but John, he was stubborn. We butted heads immediately. He sure didn't like that. I called him out when I thought he was wrong." She handed Allison a framed photograph. "And trust me, dear, he was wrong now and then."

The photo, black and white, depicted a man with dark hair and a white lab coat standing with his arm around a beautiful young woman. The woman wore a white nurse's uniform and a beaming smile, staring up at the man as if he hung the moon.

"I'm sure he was a wonderful man," Allison said, handing the photo back to her.

"Not at first. It took time. You see, I too swore that I was done with John Hattie," the woman said with a wink.

"Mrs. Hattie, it's not the—"

"The circumstances may be different, but your Jackson and my John are not so different," she said with a smile.

She shook her head emphatically. "He is not *my* Jackson, he's not my *anything*. I am simply trying to help an old friend of the family."

"Of course, dear." She patted her hand softly and walked the photo back to the desk, setting it down as she ran her fingers over the photo lovingly. "Sometimes life brings us the people we need, even if they aren't the people we think we want."

Standing up, she narrowed her eyes at the elderly woman. "Trust me, Mrs. Hattie, Jackson Lancaster isn't the person I want *or* need in my life. After tomorrow, I will never see him again."

Chapter Seven

Jackson

The hard bristles of the broom continued to move the water and baking soda around the oil-stained concrete as he scrubbed angrily at the ground. Mumbling, he tried to distract himself with the loud tunes of Whitesnake reverberating through the garage.

It had been hours since Allison had left, yet Jax was still milling about with pent-up frustration. Despite how the day had gone, he had expected her to give up and go back to Erie after putting her to work in the garage.

A small, satisfied smile slid across his lips as he replayed the day in his mind. He had taken great satisfaction in the way her cheeks colored red in anger when the oil splashed on her skirt. Watching the oil drip down her legs while she tried to keep her emotions from bubbling over had been particularly satisfying.

It was a damn shame that she irritated him so much because she had looked like a damn wet dream bent over that Ford Mustang covered in oil. Her infernal skirt left no room for imagination as it clung to her ass. There was no doubt about it. Allison Hanover was a fucking siren.

Tossing the broom against the wall, he made his way over to the counters to tidy up the remnants of the day. It seemed like he was the only Lancaster still working here, as he hadn't seen his little brother since Allison had arrived earlier that morning.

Jax was walking a fine line between extending grace to Dylan and wanting to knock his teeth out for being an irresponsible little shit. Lately, he couldn't quite figure out what was going on with him. The only thing he could be certain of was that Dylan would either be drunk at Boondocks or off making poor decisions with Donna Draper.

He picked up a stack of invoices from the counter that slipped from his grasp and scattered onto the floor. Cursing, he bent to gather them up, and that's when he noticed a few pages that didn't belong. Hidden among the mundane order sheets were drawings he had never seen before. He cursed the creaks and snaps in his hip and back as he attempted to stand back up.

Shit, he was getting old.

Holding a page up to the light, the pencil drawing captivated him. The artist had delicately captured a man hunched over what seemed to be the remains of a motorcycle. Gasping, he realized that the drawing was of himself. Setting it on the counter, he sifted through the other drawings: a bird, a dog that looked similar to his own pup, Whiskey chasing a ball, tall trees with a creek running through them. There were ten or fifteen drawings strewn across the counter, evidence Dylan had been scribbling away throughout the day.

Jax didn't know his brother even knew how to draw, let alone that he had this kind of talent. His brother had never even expressed an interest in art before.

Outside the garage, he heard a crash, accompanied by Dylan's loud muttering of curse words. Reacting quickly, Jax gathered the drawings and discreetly tucked them under the counter, concealing them from view.

Dylan stumbled through the door, stopping short when he realized Jax was standing at the counter. "Oh, hey, thought you'd be gone by now," he mumbled.

Jax scrubbed the counter with a rag and squinted at his brother. "Still cleaning up. You know I had to do my job and yours."

Dylan sighed. "Yeah, sorry about that. I had to run some errands. "He watched his brother shuffle through his bullshit excuses. He realized Dylan must think he was a goddamn idiot or a complete fool.

"Save the BS, Dyl. The only errand you ran was with a bottle at Boondocks," he snapped. "Meanwhile, I had to take care of everything here on my own all day."

Dylan smirked. "You had help."

Irritated by his brother's smug expression, Jax grumbled, "If by help you mean the city slicker, all she's done is raise my blood pressure."

Dylan chuckled. "Maybe you should just fuck her and get it over with."

"Fuck her? No way. I wouldn't touch that woman with your dick."

"Kinky!" Dylan raised his eyebrows. "Not saying you should trust her, but I can't say I'd turn down sleeping with her."

Jax glared at him, wondering why the comment bothered him as much as it did. "Well, you won't have the chance," he said firmly. "I'm going to make sure she goes home tomorrow."

"What are you going to do? Kidnap her and drop her at the edge of town?" Dylan chuckled again, pausing briefly to stare at Jax with a hint of nervousness. "You aren't actually going to kidnap her, are you?"

"Nah, that's a bit dramatic, even for me," he said, squinting his eyes. "However, I have come up with a plan."

His brother groaned. "Jax, why do I have a bad feeling about this?"

"Because you watch too much Star Wars, asshole." Jax grinned, clasping his hands together and shaking his head. "Now, Operation Free Firefly begins tomorrow."

Dylan slapped his forehead and muttered, "This is ridiculous and bound for failure."

"Have a little faith, will ya?" Honestly, he thought he'd get a bit more respect from his little brother.

"Can I just ask you something?" Dylan leaned against the counter.

"Well now, that depends on how stupid the damn question is."

"Why don't you just find out how she wants to help you? You've been struggling with the shop stuff, and we need the help. So why can't you stop being so damn stubborn just this once?"

Jax glared at his brother. "Because I can figure it out on my own. I don't need her coming in here and looking down her nose at me in her fancy suit and her expensive heels."

"Is that all this is about?" Dylan's arms flailed. "You feeling disrespected because she has more money than us? Because that's stupid."

"I don't give a shit about her money. I care about the fact she thinks she's better than us."

Jax turned to walk away, but the pounding of Dylan's fist on the counter caught his attention. "She's never once said that, Jax! Did she? As of now, all I've heard her say is that she was here to help because Dad asked her to."

Jax faced him, his nostrils flaring. "And maybe Dad should have stayed out of it," Jax said. "Maybe Dad should have trusted that I could figure it out instead of thinking I'm an idiot who can't run his store."

"Dad never said that either," Dylan mumbled.

"You know, you're real confusing, Dyl, because I thought you told me I shouldn't trust her, and now you're arguing for me to listen to her," Jax said with an angry growl.

"I'm not saying you should trust her. I *do* have a bad feeling about her, and I don't know why." He shrugged.

Jax chuckled. "Because you're a damn conspiracy theorist, Dyl, you don't trust anyone." Exhaling, he put his hands on his hips. "But *you* should trust me. Why does it feel like no one in this family thinks I can do this?"

Dylan rolled his eyes and shook his head, running his hands through his hair. "That's because you always just assume we all think the worst of you."

"Yeah, well, at least I know better," Jax said. "I never have to be surprised when people get disappointed. Unlike you, you're a walking disappointment and don't even realize it yet!" It was a low blow, he knew that. From the look on his brother's face, he should take it back and apologize, but there was no stopping him once it was out. "What exactly are you doing with your life, anyway?"

"It's none of your goddamn business," Dylan said, his voice raising over the music playing on the radio.

"Bullshit," Jax grunted, stepping toward him. "You're my little brother, you work for me, and all I see is you coming home drunk, doing nothing with your life, skipping out on work. Hell, I don't even know where you disappear to half the time."

"I told you, it's none of your concern." Dylan turned to leave.

Jax followed him to the door. "Is it Donna? Is that where you keep running off to? Cuz I told you that girl is trouble, Dyl."

He pivoted to face him. "You think I don't know that? You think I enjoy being Blake's hand-me-down? Just—" He paused, staring off into the darkness of the garage. "It's not all about her, man. Just leave it alone."

Before he could stop him, Dylan had rushed out of the garage, the door slamming closed behind him. Jax stood alone in the darkened garage, contemplating everything his brother had said. Storm clouds loomed overhead, a rain that had been threatening for days, but none of that compared to the storm inside his mind.

Whiskey sat at Jax's feet as he sipped his beer on the couch, engrossed in a rerun of Survivor playing on the television. Although it was Jax's favorite episode, it also was the most annoying one. His sister's text interrupted his viewing, informing him she had caught up to the same scene. Every Saturday night, they had made it a ritual to watch Survivor together and exchange thoughts via text. Even Blake had joined in on the action, now that he was being coerced into watching with Sam. They were currently watching episode ten of Survivor Caramoan.

Sam

"Hold up, bro"

Sam

Best Malcolm line on Survivor EVER!!!

Jax

classic line but shit move

Jax shook his head, observing the man, and move as it played out on the screen. The man in question, Malcolm, uttered his famous line, "Hold up, bro," mentioned by his sister, and held up his immunity idol. It was a classic Survivor move. However, instead of targeting the nerd, Cochran, who should have been voted out initially, the idiot targeted some putz, a move which resulted in Cochran winning the entire season. Proof that classic lines don't equal winning moves, Malcolm.

Blake

What am I missing?

Sam

Jax is just jealous because Malcolm has better hair than him

Jax

Trust me B, you'll understand in a few weeks.

Jax

Dude just blew up his game

As the episode winded down, he clicked out of the group chat and hovered over his sister's name. Perhaps it was time to talk to Sam about Dylan's behavior lately. Deciding he had nothing to lose, he clicked on her number and waited while it rang. She picked up immediately.

"Hey loser, you don't have to be a hater, you know. His hair isn't that much better than yours," she teased.

"Very funny, sis. The man literally lost that season because of that move. You know that, right?" he said.

"Did you really call to talk to me about a game that was over ten years ago?" she asked, pausing for a beat. "Or do you have something else on your mind?"

He sighed before speaking again. "I wanted to talk about Dylan. Is he still texting you?"

"Mostly in the mornings, but it's been a lot of talk about his breakfast lately. I was actually going to ask you about him," she said. "Even Dylan isn't that excited about food that he has nothing else to talk about."

"Yeah..." He let the word draw out for a moment. "I don't think things are going well with him."

"What's going on?" she asked, her voice lowering.

"He's drinking," he said. He tried to brush it off with a laugh, not wanting to cause his sister additional anxiety.

"He's always drinking. I swear him and Blake made that a pastime," she said, and Jax heard Blake protest in the background, and he chuckled softly to himself.

"Yeah, not that kind of drinking. It's not a Friday night thing, it's daily. He's stumbling home most nights, when he's not crawling out of Double D's bed," he said, clenching as he waited for the response.

"Tell me he's not?" she whispered into the phone. He heard rustling as if she had gotten up and left the room. "He's sleeping with Donna?" He heard a door close. "Sorry, I didn't want to talk about this in front of Blake. Why would he be sleeping with Donna?"

"He says he's got nothing better to do," he said with a snort.

"There are a lot of other things he could do besides Donna Draper, Jax," she said, but this time, her voice was less calm. Her tone had elevated in a manner that he recognized from his growing up with her as annoyance.

"I've told him that, but he's not exactly talking to me civilly. Hell, I can't even get him to show up to work most days," he said, bracing for his sister's response.

He heard her sigh. "Damn, Jax, I didn't know it was this bad. He seemed distant, but I just thought he missed us."

"I do think he's a bit lost without both you and Blake, but this feels like a lot more. He's struggling," Jax admitted. It felt like a load off his shoulders to say it out loud, to acknowledge that his brother needed help and he didn't know what to do about it. He missed his sister, and even though she was the baby, she always took care of them. Sam would know what to do.

"Do you want me to talk to him?" Sam asked.

He closed his eyes and pinched his nose with his fingers, contemplating the idea. "I don't know if he'll listen yet," Jax said, and that was the truth. He didn't know if their brother would just hang up on her. Dylan sure as hell wasn't listening to him—and he was right there in his face. He paused for a moment before changing the subject. "Hey, did you know Dylan draws?" he asked.

Sam sounded surprised. "He does?"

"Yeah, I found some drawings in the shop. I'm pretty sure they're his. Pretty good stuff, too."

"No, I did not know. But you know how private Dylan is about everything," Sam sighed. "Maybe I'll see what I can do in our texts tomorrow. I won't mention that we spoke, but just pry a bit about how things are going there."

"Don't ask him about Allison," Jax quickly warned, the mention of her name stirring up mixed emotions.

Sam laughed. "Oh really? What's the story there?"

Jax cursed inwardly at his slip-up. "Nothing. No story. After tomorrow, she's going back to Erie," he said, trying to end the conversation.

"What's happening tomorrow?" Sam asked.

"Operation Free Firefly," he said with a bubbly voice that made him crinkle his nose immediately. He was probably giving his sister too much information.

"Jackson, what the hell is that?" Her voice sounded like his mother's used to when she was angry at him. "Or do I even want to know?"

"Best not to ask, sis. Plausible deniability."

Chapter Eight

Allison

Allison checked her reflection in the rearview mirror, pinching her red-stained lips together. She needed to gather the courage to get out of the car and march into Lancaster's Auto Shop. Today, she was bound and determined to demand Jackson let her teach him what she had come here to do. She planned to head back to Erie before the sun had even set in the west, ending this weekend as some sort of success.

With steely-eyed determination, she exited the car, pushing the door shut with her butt. Although she didn't have her favorite Louboutin heels today, her trusty backups would have to do. Striding into the garage, she made her way straight to the office where Jackson was sitting at his desk.

Goddamn, he looked good in glasses. *Focus, Allison.*

Allison quickly refocused and stared directly into Jackson's eyes. He looked up at her, peeling his glasses down his nose with a smile. She opened her mouth to speak, but he cut her off. "Morning, Allison. Glad you finally made it." His voice was calm and polite, lacking the edge she had heard the previous times she had dealt with him. "I've been waiting for you."

"What?" Allison stuttered, surprised by his unexpected demeanor.

"Actually, I expected you twenty minutes ago," Jackson said, frowning as he glanced at his watch. "We've got work to do, and we're already late."

Allison shook her head. There was no way she was working in the garage again today. "Work? Wait, what are you talking about?"

"The books!" Jackson held up one of his ledgers, looking at her as if she should have known. Her mouth dropped open in disbelief.

"The books?" she said. "The books!" she nearly shouted. "Now you want to do the books?"

"Alright, we can wait til after I run my errands." Without hesitation, Jackson stood up, tossing his annoyingly attractive glasses onto the desk, and grabbing the keys to his truck. He walked to the door and turned back to her. "Aren't you coming?"

Allison barely had time to understand what he was saying before he left the office and was halfway out of the garage. She hurried to catch up with him. "Jackson, wait, where are we going?"

He grinned. "I have errands to run. Can you teach me what I need to know while we're out?" Opening the door, he gestured for her to step outside. "Ladies first."

Had she entered an alternate universe? Had aliens suddenly invaded earth and replaced Jackson with a pod person?

He approached his truck and opened the passenger side door. "Up you go, wouldn't want you to break another heel." She hesitated, looking at his hand as if it was a foreign object.

Shaking her head, she closed her eyes as she spoke. "Jackson, I'm not even sure I can teach you anything in the truck. We need to go back inside and examine your books and—"

"Oh, come on now, Allison. I have faith in you. I'm sure you're a great teacher." Just as she was about to object, he reached down and effortlessly lifted her into the truck. "There we go. Don't forget to buckle up. Safety first, always." He turned around and whistled, and a large dog came bounding through the wooded trees toward the car, running purposefully toward them—directly at her.

Feeling a sense of dread, Allison shrank into her seat. "Um—Jackson, this would probably be a good time for me to tell you that..." Her voice trailed off as the dog jumped into the truck, leaping over her lap and settling into the seat beside her. Jackson quickly shut the door, leaving her alone with the dog. She turned toward it, feeling herself tremble, and finished her sentence with a wavering voice. "I don't really get along with dogs."

The driver's side door swung open, allowing Jackson to climb into the truck. She could sense that perhaps all his macho behavior he had just displayed had caused him some discomfort as he popped a few aspirins into his mouth and swallowed. Once settled in his seat, he announced, "Just going to make a couple of stops." He turned toward her and smiled. "Now, start my lessons, teach!"

As Jackson spoke, the dog's breath warmed Allison's face, its snout hovering near her cheek. With her stomach churning, her words came out slightly quicker than she intended. "Does it need to be this close to my face? Should I be worried?"

He seemed surprised by her tone as he chuckled, brushing off her anxious behavior. "Worried about what? Whiskey's about the nicest dog you'll ever meet."

She hesitated, feeling her racing heart pounding in her chest. "Yes, well, I don't meet many dogs," she admitted, swallowing nervously. Her hands clasped anxiously in her lap as she continued, "As I was trying to tell you earlier, I don't really get along with dogs."

"That's nonsense. Everyone gets along with Whiskey." He affectionately patted the dog's head, causing it to slobber and lick his hands. Allison couldn't help but shiver in disgust at the germ exchange happening in front of her. "Come on, boy, show Firefly how much you like her."

She turned quickly toward Jackson to insist against this. "That's not necess—" But before she could protest, the dog's tongue slipped inside her mouth, catching her by surprise. The taste of saliva overwhelmed her senses, and she squealed in shock. Quickly, she brought her hand to her mouth and pulled away.

Amidst her disgust, Jackson remained unfazed. "See that there, that's love. He don't kiss just anyone. I think he really likes you."

As she scrubbed at her lips, trying to get the taste of whatever the dog had last eaten out of her mouth, he pulled into their stop and jumped out of the truck. "I'll be right back, you two. Play nice,

Allison," he said with a wink. She hated this man with every fiber of her being.

Once alone in the truck, she glanced at the dog and frowned. "Look, you just stay over there, and I'll stay here. And no more kissing," she warned, holding her hands between them. The dog whined softly, laying his head in her lap, and Allison wasn't sure what to do. He was getting hair all over her black skirt. "No, move back to your side," she said, trying to ask polity but hoping that her firm tone would show that dog that she meant business. Apparently, the dog didn't speak her language. He simply cuddled closer and exhaled a loud breath and closed his eyes.

She sat as still as she could, staring out the window as she waited for Jackson to return. He sure was taking his sweet old time.

A man walked past her door, staring at her with a flirty smile. "Hey there, gorgeous," he said through the open window. "I don't think I've seen you in town before."

"I'm not interested," Allison said with a loud exhale and turned away. Could she not get one moment of peace?

"Hey, I'm just trying to be friendly." He stepped closer to the truck and put his hand into the open window. Suddenly, the dog sat up, growling like an angry mutt, before letting out a loud bark.

Allison jumped and sat back firmly in her seat as the man moved away from the window. "Damn, Whiskey, I was just saying hi," the man complained as he walked away from the truck.

Allison looked down at the dog as it continued to growl, leaning over her, his head out the window as it watched until the man was far enough away from the truck for his liking. Once the dog was satisfied the man was no longer a threat, it climbed back to the center of the seat and laid down, resting his head in her lap again. Allison's heart was pounding in her chest, unsure what to make of the dog that was now calmly licking its paws beside her. Perhaps there was some benefit to a dog after all.

Suddenly, the truck door opened, and Jackson tossed an enormous bag of food toward them. Clumps of food spilled out onto the floor and into her lap. "Damn."

"What in the..." The dog was in her lap now, heavy and full of all that hair as it tried to clean up morsels clinging to her shirt and between her cleavage. The dog's tongue was warm against her chest, causing her to squeeze her eyes shut as she screeched loudly, pushing him away. "Get him off me!" she shouted.

Her door opened and Jackson pulled on the dog's leash, causing it to jump down out of the truck. "You alright, Firefly?" he asked.

She opened her eyes and felt herself flush as she looked down at the state of her clothing. Her top two buttons had come undone, revealing her white lace bra covered in dog food. Quickly, she reached for her shirt and pulled it closed, staring back at him angrily. "I'm fine. What the hell were you thinking?"

Jackson grinned sheepishly. "I tripped. Sometimes my knee gives out." His eyes felt like they were burning into her skin as he stared at her chest. She narrowed her gaze and glared at him, causing him to step back out of her sight. She adjusted her clothes while he walked back to his side of the truck and Whiskey jumped up, returning to his seat. "I'll just dump the rest of this in the back and we'll be on our way."

"Are we going back to the garage now?" she asked.

Jackson shrugged. "We still have a few more places to go. But maybe we can talk about gross profit margins on the way to the trail."

"The trail?" Her voice squeaked in annoyance.

He popped his head back into the truck. "Yeah, I gotta walk Whiskey. As you can tell, he's got a lot of pent-up energy." He disappeared again, stepping behind the truck, and she sighed in resignation.

Finally, after securing the rest of the dog food, he hopped back into his seat and set off for the next destination. "Alright, fine. Gross profit margins, so I'm guessing you know something about them?" she asked.

"Just so you're aware, I'm not a total idiot. I'm just self-taught. I'm not tech savvy so my computer and I have beef, and I don't always understand all those fancy terms you keep throwing around, but it don't mean that I don't understand what some of them words mean already. So, you don't have to treat me like a total moron."

She nodded and turned back to face the road. "Fine, well then, typically, your gross profit margins should range between twenty percent and thirty percent for a business such as yours. This will vary depending on how well you can manage your costs and pricing strategy."

Jackson shrugged. "So, what I charge for labor, right?"

"It's a bit more than that," she said with a laugh. "But yes, labor is part of that."

"Cool, so as long as I set the right price for labor and the cost of my service, that will affect my revenue and gross profit?" He smirked, and Allison hated that her stomach swooped just from the way his eyes crinkled when he smiled. "Look at me, sounding all smart and shit."

She rolled her eyes. "Don't go getting cocky. You knew one thing and only barely part of it," she said. "We really should go back to your office, sit down, and look at your books."

"Slow down, sweetheart. Stop being so anxious to get into my books. I'm not that easy," he said with a frustratingly handsome smirk. "I told you, after the errands." The truck slowed down next to a patch of trees near a trailhead.

"How long are you going to be?" she asked. "I'll just wait here."

He laughed. "No can do, Allison. Can't just leave you in the truck. Besides, we can learn on the trail." With a smile, he opened the door and jumped out of the truck, groaning slightly as he stepped down. He turned back to her, his mask firmly back on his face. "Think of it like a field trip." Suddenly, that smile and crinkle weren't so attractive anymore.

She pushed the door open and stepped down onto the rocky ground beneath her, the heel of her shoe digging into the dirt. Flustered and annoyed, she reminded herself that Jackson Lancaster would not defeat her, despite his frustrating behavior and his unfortunately devastatingly good looks.

She straightened her skirt and followed him down the trail, occasionally hobbling when her heel got stuck in the muddy dirt. As she walked, she closed her eyes and envisioned her apartment back home, imagining a relaxing bath and losing herself in one of her favorite romance novels by Natalie Murray.

He interrupted her. "So, tell me how I balance my finances each month without messing everything up." Startled, she glanced over at Jackson, who was already looking at her.

She tripped over her own feet and tried to recover gracefully. "There's a simple formula for that: A=L+E."

"I hope you know I failed algebra." He chuckled.

She responded matter-of-factly, "Assets equals liabilities plus equity."

He let out an exasperated sigh. "I didn't ask for a Spanish lesson. Can you explain it in English, please?"

She tried to simplify her explanation. "Assets are everything you own, like tools and equipment, even the cars you work on. Your liabilities are the bills you owe, such as loans. And equity is what you have left after subtracting your liabilities from your assets." She stared back at him, gauging his expression. "Does that make sense?"

"You know, you're a pretty good teacher," he remarked as his dog ran ahead toward a small creek bed. "Whiskey, get back here!" he hollered after the dog.

They followed the dog, stopping at the edge of the creek. "I think we should get back to the truck," she said anxiously, reaching down to adjust her heels. "The ground isn't exactly dry back here."

"I think we should give Whiskey a bit more time, he's just having fun." Jackson watched his dog bouncing in the creek playfully. All she could think about was how wet his fur was getting. "Besides, we've accomplished so much already."

"Jackson, we have barely covered the surface of what you need to know. I've taught you a few terms, that's all," she tried to explain. "We need to go back to the office."

Before she could move, Whiskey playfully jumped up and pushed her backward, causing her to stumble and slip against the mossy rocks beneath her feet. She felt her shoe lodge against something firm, and then she tumbled into the cold water. The dog leapt into her lap. The cool stream rushed past her, splashing into her hair.

"Whiskey, off!" Jackson shouted, but she was sure she heard a laugh beneath his words. The dog jumped off of her and ran toward Jackson. Her hands fell to the water in defeat. Anger and frustration bubbling just under the surface beneath her soaked clothing. "If I had known we were going for a swim, I would have dressed for it."

"Do I look like I'm dressed for swimming?" she growled, staring up at him, water dripping from her forehead.

He extended his hand, looking down at her with a frown. "I'm just trying to help, Allison."

"I think you've done quite enough of that, thank you," she responded. Refusing his offer of help, she pushed herself up off the ground. "If you don't mind, I would like to go back to the garage now."

"But I'm not done with my errands yet," he said.

"I don't care about your goddamn errands, Jackson. I'm soaked, I'm tired, and I want to go home," she snapped in frustration.

"Well, sweetheart, don't let me delay you!" he answered with a grin. "I'll help get you home right away."

She narrowed her eyes and stalked after him with frustration as they walked back to the truck in silence. She would rather spend all day kissing the dog than another minute with Jackson Lancaster.

Pulling into the garage, Allison felt a sense of relief at the sight of her own vehicle parked outside the building. All she wanted was to head back to the hotel, take a shower, and unwind. Her patience with Jackson Lancaster and his issues had worn thin. She had given it the old college try, but that was over.

Stepping out of the truck, she was startled when the dog jumped down behind her and rushed toward Dylan Lancaster. "Oh, there you are," he said, emerging from the garage just as they pulled in. "I've been holding down the fort all day. Where have you been?"

Jackson was unloading dog food from the truck as she walked toward her car. "I was picking up more dog food," Jackson said to his brother.

"But you just bought some yesterday," Dylan said. Allison paused and turned toward Jackson, caught red-handed with his hand in the cookie jar.

"I, uh..." he stammered, meeting Allison's gaze.

With a tilt of her head, Allison raised her brow. "You just bought dog food?"

Jackson chuckled. "I guess I forgot."

"What do you take me for?" Allison said, unable to hide her irritation. Jackson shrugged, prompting her to lash out. "You're such an asshole. Dragging me around all day, pretending to care about what I had to teach you."

Jackson raised his hands in front of him. "Why does it matter to you, anyway?"

Bracing her hands on her hips, she closed her eyes. "It doesn't. I don't care what you do anymore." When she opened her eyes, she stared him down, before turning to her car and climbing in. She sped as far away as she could get from Jackson Lancaster.

Later that night, nestled in her corner booth at Linda's Diner, she stabbed at the lettuce on her plate. How dare Jackson Lancaster play games with her all day!

Contemplating cutting her losses and returning home, she couldn't shake the feeling that it would be a defeat she wasn't ready to accept. The game with Jackson was becoming personal to her, and she wasn't quite willing to lose yet. Staring at her plate, she stabbed her fork into the lettuce once more.

A voice interrupted her thoughts. "Wow, you look as bad as I feel today." Looking up, she found the waitress, Jamila, holding the check.

"Sorry, it's been a really long day," she groaned. "I made out with a dog and got thrown in a creek."

Jamila stared at her. "Wow, and I thought serving food to a few perverts who told me I had nice tits was a bad day," the girl said, sinking into the bench on the other side of her table.

Sighing heavily, Allison felt the need to unload her disappointment at how badly the day had unfolded. "I really thought today was going to go differently," she said instead.

"It still can," Jamila offered, piquing Allison's curiosity. "But please tell me you have something else to wear besides those business suits."

Eager for a change of pace, she lifted an eyebrow. "I don't, but what did you have in mind?"

"What size do you wear? Because I think I might have something that would fit you." The girl grinned devilishly, and Allison was suddenly open to whatever the waitress had in mind.

Chapter Nine

Jackson

Jax leaned over the pool table, focusing intently as he lined up the ball with his pool stick. "And then she fell in the creek," he casually mentioned, shrugging before taking his shot. The balls scattered across the table, and a solid blue ball smoothly sank into the corner pocket. Standing up, he tried to ignore the pain in his hip. Carrying all that dog food and acting like a fool today came at a price.

Dylan took a sip of his beer. "So, she just went home?"

He scanned the table, picking up his beer bottle. "That's it. Operation Free Firefly was a success," Jax confirmed, preparing for his next shot. "You almost blew it when you blurted out that I already bought dog food," Jax said with a chuckle.

"I don't know. That might have helped your cause. I thought she was going to murder you," he snorted. "She doesn't seem to be a fan of yours."

Missing his next shot, he walked over to his stool and sat down. "Shame too, she was smokin' hot."

"Ah, finally admitting it now?" Dylan said, bending over to take his shot. "Thought she was untouchable, not even with my dick. Wasn't that what you said?"

Jax jokingly flicked his middle finger in the air toward his brother. "Fuck off, Dyl." They bantered back and forth, their attention shifting to the game at hand.

Jax waited until his brother was distracted before he switched the topic. He seemed to be in a good mood tonight, so he took his chance. "So, the other night while cleaning up the shop, I stumbled upon some interesting drawings." He lined up his next shot, maintaining his focus on the yellow ball.

Once he had made the shot successfully, Jax looked up to see Dylan staring at him. "You went through my things?" Dylan asked, crossing his arms against his chest.

Jax felt the need to clarify himself. "No, I found them under the invoices. Relax, Dylan, no need to get so defensive."

An uncomfortable silence followed before Dylan responded, "I'd rather not discuss it, and don't touch my stuff in the future." Jax, concentrating on his next shot, missed the corner pocket.

He stood up and walked back to his stool. "They were good, bro." This caught his brother's attention, causing his eyes to snap toward him. "We just didn't know you were interested in that kind of thing."

You know when you're watching a movie and you can see that moment when a character makes a pivotal mistake and you're yelling at the screen, "Hey idiot, don't do that!" This was that moment.

"We? Did you talk to Sam about this? Are the two of you talking about me behind my back?"

Jax closed his eyes and let out a groan. "Dyl, it's not like that."

Anger flared in Dylan's eyes. "Then tell me what it's like. Because I thought it was odd that suddenly my sister is asking all sorts of questions this morning." With a forceful shove, he sent his pool stick crashing onto the table, scattering the balls in all directions. "Stupid of me to think maybe it was cuz she missed me, when all this time it was just the two of you conspiring behind my back out of some bullshit mistrust you have in me."

"No one mistrusts you, Dylan."

"Bullshit!" he shouted. The tension escalated as Dylan's outburst drew attention from those around them. Jax stood and walked toward him, and Dylan backed away. "You both think I'm a fuck-up."

"I've never said that," Jax said, standing taller as his brother cowered in front of him. "I know your sister doesn't believe that either." Dylan glared at him and stared off toward the bar. "Dylan, listen to me," Jax continued. "I just think you're going through a rough patch right now. I know things have been hard since Blake left."

"Don't do that. Don't pretend to understand me, Jax. Just don't," Dylan replied, his brother's hands on his hips and his chin lowered toward his chest.

Jax sighed. "Then talk to me. Help me understand."

For a moment, it seemed like Dylan might open up to him, his eyes softening. However, a sudden commotion behind them disrupted the discussion, and as soon as Dylan looked away, Jax knew the moment was gone. "I'm gonna head out," Dylan said.

Jax exhaled, trying to salvage the situation. "Can we just—"

"Let it go, Jax," Dylan interrupted firmly. Disheartened, Jax watched as Dylan walked away to join Donna at the bar, prompting Jax to toss his pool stick onto the table in defeat.

Hours after Dylan had left Jax alone at the bar, he sat in his booth listening to the loud music playing overhead, a familiar Blake Shelton song about drinking beer. Jax, who was nursing his own beer with his foot propped on the bench in the corner booth, glanced over to see two women at the bar. He recognized Jamila Jones, a waitress at Linda's diner. There just weren't many dark-skinned women in Titusville. She was friendly, if not a bit too talkative, for his taste.

Beside her stood a woman in skin-tight jeans and a snug polka-dotted tank top, showcasing her creamy white skin and long curly red hair cascading down her back. Jax couldn't help but imagine running his fingers through her fiery locks as she screamed out his name in the throes of passion. Maybe it had been too long since he'd gotten laid.

Determined to improve on his awful day, he stumbled toward the bar to introduce himself. "Jamila Jones, it's been a while," he greeted with a smile. "Gonna introduce me to your beautiful friend?"

Jamila replied with a grin, "Well, look what the cat dragged in. It would be my pleasure to—"

Jax turned to see a familiar pair of icy blue eyes. "Allison," he muttered.

"Jackson," she said, with a touch of venom lacing her words.

"Do you two know each other?" Jamila asked with a hint of amusement.

"Jackson is my reason for being in town," Allison stated firmly, locking eyes with Jamila.

The dark-skinned woman opened her mouth and then smiled widely. "Oh." A moment of clarity passed between the two women as she exhaled. "Oh!"

"I thought you went back to Erie," Jax grumbled, gesturing to Rusty for a new beer. Apparently, he was going to need a lot more alcohol tonight.

Allison appeared to fake a smile. "No, you *assumed* I went back to Erie. Jamila has convinced me to stick around a little while longer."

"Has she now?" He turned toward the waitress. "Well, I'll have to be sure and remember that the next time I stop by the diner." He locked eyes with the woman. "If I forget your tip next time, remember this conversation."

Jamila's eyebrow shot up in intrigue before she turned to Allison. "Girl, now I totally understand what you were saying."

Allison shrugged and held up her hand. "He's a delight, right?"

"What are you talking about?" he questioned the girls, who just giggled and ignored him. Rusty slid a beer between them, and Jax picked it up.

"What am I getting you, ladies?" the bartender asked.

Jamila immediately answered. "I'll have the usual Russ."

He nodded and went to work on making her some sort of pink concoction, then looked up at Allison. "What about you, Red?"

Allison bit her lip while staring down at the menu, peeling the sticky pages apart. "I don't really drink, so I'm not sure."

Jax chuckled under his breath. "That explains a lot."

She turned toward him with a pinched brow. "What is that supposed to mean?"

Jax shrugged. "Nothin', you're just wound tight."

"Excuse me!" she shot back, her voice elevated over the loud music.

Jax laughed and tilted his head toward her. "I rest my case." He gestured to Rusty. "Get the little lady a vodka spritz."

"Oh, Jax, nice choice," Jamila chimed in.

Jax bowed his head with a flick of his wrist and grinned. "I do know my alcoholic drinks, J." He then looked down at Jamila's drink and frowned. "But whatever that is, that's gonna give you a headache in the morning."

She hummed and shook her head. "I like em' sweet, Jaxxy."

"Too much sugar makes your teeth rot," he growled, unimpressed with her umbrella-topped drink, as he turned to walk back to his table.

Jamila shrilled behind him, "Don't leave now, I was just starting to enjoy the conversation." Before he could stop her, she was pressed against his back. "Don't tell me you are still hiding out in that darkened corner?"

"I like my dark corner, J. Everyone leaves me the hell alone," he grumbled, limping back toward his booth and sliding into his seat as he kicked his foot up onto the chair. But before he could enjoy his beer, Jamila and Allison were already making their way over toward him, adding more imposition to his already bad day.

Not only was his brother angry at him, but Operation Free Firefly had failed. Despite Allison looking like sex in denim, she was supposed to have left his tiny town. Yet here she was, sliding into his private hiding spot at his beloved Boondocks.

Nothing was sacred anymore.

"I don't recall the invite," he grumbled as they sat down.

Jamila shook her head and laughed. "Ignore Mr. Grumpy Pants. No one should go this long without company."

"Dylan just left ten minutes ago. Well, that's barely enough time to jerk off..." He paused as he made eye contact with the redhead across the table. "I happen to enjoy being alone," he corrected.

"Apparently," she said dryly, sipping her drink, her face suddenly puckering as she swallowed.

He chuckled. "You okay there, Firefly?" Jamila stared between the two of them, perplexed.

"I'm fine," she said, taking another drink. This time, she swallowed a bigger gulp, impressing him with her sheer determination until she came up sputtering.

"Easy, you might want to slow down," Jax warned as she slammed her empty glass on the table.

"I'll take another one of those," she demanded.

Jamila and Jax exchanged uneasy glances before Jamila got up from the table. "It's your hangover, girlfriend."

Left alone with Allison, Jax nervously stared at the graffiti scribbled on the wood of the table. "So, uh, you decided to stay, huh?"

She snorted loudly. "You really think that bullshit you pulled today was going to run me off?" She leaned across the table and locked eyes with him. "I eat assholes like you for breakfast."

"Alright then," he said with a shake of his head, leaning back against the booth and resting his arms along the top of the bench. "So, then Allison Hanover, tell me how you really feel."

Her eyes widened. "You don't want to know how I really feel."

"Sure, I do," he said with a shrug. "I ain't got nothin' better to do tonight. Besides, I bet you've been dying to tell me off."

"Honestly?" She narrowed her eyes. "I think you're just really good at playing an asshole. But I think maybe that's all an act."

"Is that so?" His smile slipped, unsure of where she was going with this.

"You act like you're too stupid to understand half the stuff I tell you, but I'm not even sure about that." She sat back in her booth, making him feel uncomfortable as she watched him closely.

"Then what exactly do you think you're here for if I've got it all so figured out? Cuz my dad wouldn't be on your ass if I was so fucking smart, now, would he?"

"Oh, I don't think you have a damn thing figured out, but you're too stubborn to listen to anyone who's willing to help you," she countered, crossing her arms against her chest. "What I haven't figured out is if you just like being an ass or if your ego is just getting in your own way. Either way, I doubt you're that different from any other guy I've met. You meet one asshole, you've met them all."

When she had finished speaking, she was panting. She had barely taken a breath from her rant and her eyes were dancing from the glow of the bar lights. Damn, she was beautiful. "Do you feel better now?" He chuckled, noticing how her eyes softened when she looked back at him.

She bit her lip before a small smile tipped upward on her mouth. "Maybe," she said.

Jamila returned to the table with her drink and sat down, staring at them. "What did I miss?"

Jax nodded toward the woman on the other side of the table. "Allison called me an egotistical asshole."

"I did not." Allison laughed with her hand over her mouth. "Well, maybe I did."

Jamila groaned. "I miss all the fun."

Three hours later, Jax found himself standing outside the bar in front of his truck as Jamila waved goodbye to Allison and hopped into her Ford Fiesta. He watched Allison begin to walk down the sidewalk and hollered after her. "Hey, Firefly."

She turned toward him and responded playfully, "Hey, asshole."

"Where are you headed?" he asked. It seemed like the polite thing to ask a woman on a Sunday night when said woman was heading out on her own after imbibing on a few alcoholic beverages.

"I'm staying at Hattie's BnB. It's only a couple of blocks away," Allison said, pointing toward the old hotel as she swayed lightly on her feet.

"I can drop you off," he said, gesturing toward his truck. She stared at him with apprehension. "Come on, I don't bite. Besides, I'm not that big of an asshole to let you walk home after a couple vodka spritzers," he said, hoping to reassure her.

"I think I can take care of myself," Allison firmly stated, like the stubborn redhead he knew her to be.

"I don't doubt that at all." He grinned. "But I also wasn't raised to let a woman walk home alone from a bar at night." Gesturing for her to join him, he added, "Humor me, please?"

Resigned, Allison sighed and followed him to the truck. "I'm only agreeing because my feet hurt, and I don't want to walk tonight."

"Of course." He laughed as he climbed into his truck.

They settled in, and Allison adjusted her seatbelt. "You do realize I'm still coming to your shop tomorrow?"

Jax nodded. "I was pretty sure of that, yes." He drove off toward Mrs. Hattie's, the sound of Loverboy's, "This Could Be the Night" playing softly on the radio. The dark and empty streets of the town at the late hour made Jax grateful he had convinced Allison to let him drive her back to her hotel.

He heard her shuffle beside him. "You aren't going to throw a fish at me or something, are you?" she asked, twisting her hands together in her lap.

"What?" he turned toward her in confusion.

"Look, I get it. You don't want me here. But today, with the dog food and the creek, I'm not giving up on teaching you, even if you've given up on learning. I don't care what you throw at me or try to do to scare me off, Jackson. I'm going to do what your dad asked me to do." She stopped talking, her chest moving up and down rapidly as she continued to stare at him.

He pulled over to the curb in front of Hattie's and parked. "Allison, I'm not going to throw a fish at you." Her shoulders relaxed. "Look, maybe I've been a tad difficult."

"I'm sorry, what?" she snorted, covering her mouth immediately.

"Okay, perhaps I've been a bit more than that," he agreed. "And I'm not saying I am suddenly happy or excited that my father sent you here. That's just me being honest." He stared at his hands that were still gripping the steering wheel. "But that's not exactly your fault either, and I might have taken that out on you, and I apologize for that."

She stared at him, dumbfounded. "Wow. That is..." Shaking her head, she managed a smile. "Did you just apologize?"

"Alright, I think you've had enough for one night. Get out." He chuckled.

"You're just a big softie, aren't you?" she said as she opened her door.

"Hey!" he shouted before she could shut the door. "Don't let anyone hear you say something like that. You'll ruin my reputation."

"Sure, Jackson!" she said with a wink, stumbling slightly on her feet as she let the door slam shut behind her.

And perhaps, just perhaps, Jax watched her walk all the way to the front door that night, *for her own safety*, of course. Not because he was watching the way her ass swished from side to side, or how her hair shined a bright crimson red in the moonlight. It was clearly for her protection and nothing else.

Because Allison Hanover was still a giant pain in the ass.

Chapter Ten

Allison

Allison woke up on Monday morning with a slight headache but a new determination. She had agreed to meet Jamila at the local shopping center to buy new clothes. There was no way she was going to get away with wearing the suit and heels she had brought with her. Besides, she was tired of washing her clothes every night.

Despite the small truce she had made with Jackson last night, she didn't trust him to stop being difficult. If there was one thing she had always been taught, it was to dress for the job. And right now, she needed to dress for combat.

Standing outside the store, she waited for her new friend. She heard a whistle and looked up just as Jamila approached her. "Glad to see you're still on your feet after the way you downed those drinks last night."

"It's gonna take a lot more than a couple of vodka spritzers to knock me down," she said with a shrug.

"Seems like you and Jax were starting to thaw last night." The girl bumped her shoulder with hers as they entered the store. "Tell me there's more to the story there."

She shook her head and crinkled her brow. "There really isn't a story. He gets on my nerves. I annoy him. The end."

"Please, with the way you two were looking at each other last night, I was pretty sure he wanted to get on more than your nerves." Jamila wriggled her eyebrows playfully.

"No, definitely not." She chuckled. "He is just as anxious for me to leave town as I am to go home."

"Trust me, that look he was giving you did not say, 'leave me alone.'. That boy wanted your attention." Allison ran her hands over the racks of clothing, most of which were not her style, but she was sure she would find something she could work with.

"Look, whatever way he was looking, doesn't matter. I just want to do what I came here to do and go home," she said, putting the dress back on the rack.

"And that requires a new wardrobe?" Jamila asked with a cheeky grin.

"It requires something I can wear that I won't mind getting covered in grease and oil," she said with a sigh.

Jamila's mouth formed an O before she slyly replied, "Kinky."

"Because he works in an auto shop, Jamila, not for sexual purposes," she said, trying not to conjure up images of Jackson Lancaster covered in sweat and grease.

The woman sighed with a frown. "You really are wasting a hunk of a man."

"I'll just have to be okay with that." She shrugged. "Besides, I kind of sort of have someone back in Erie." She regretted even bringing Chip up. It almost felt like a defense mechanism to get Jamila to stop talking. But now that it was out, she braced herself for what she knew was going to be twenty questions from her friend.

"Kind of sort of? What does that even mean?" Jamila frowned. "Boyfriend? Lover? Benefits situation?"

Allison teased her lip roughly with her teeth. Chip wasn't actually any of those things to her. They weren't dating, and he definitely wasn't her boyfriend. "He's kind of my boss."

"Oh Lord, you're so messy, child." The woman shook her head and slid over to the rack of clothes beside her. "Did anyone ever tell you not to shit where you eat?"

"Yeah, we used to date before I got the job at the firm. I don't know. He's one of those things you try to quit, but can't," Allison groaned.

"Yeah girl, well, most of those things are bad for you, too. Like cigarettes or heroin." Jamila's voice was firm and confident, and Allison knew she wasn't wrong. "I know you're smarter than that."

Allison sighed. "He's also a pretty big asshole."

"So, you have a type, then." Jamila laughed.

Allison thought about it. Jackson wasn't like Chip, though. Sure, he was arrogant and acted like a jerk, but Chip was mean and cruel. From what she had observed of Jackson, he wasn't like that. Not that she was defending Jackson's behavior, of course.

Allison stood in the middle of the aisle, dumbfounded by the internal struggle she was currently having regarding Chip Ryder and Jackson Lancaster.

"Earth to Allison." She looked up to see her friend staring at her.

"Sorry, I was literally just standing here trying to decide who was the bigger asshole, Jackson or Chip," she said with a shake of her head.

"Who won?" Jamila asked.

"Chip, by a long shot," she said, as her friend looked on ominously.

"Ooh girl, that is not a good sign for your future," she said, shaking her head.

Pulling a few items from the rack, Allison walked toward the fitting room. "I didn't actually plan on having a future with him, honestly. He's always been just a means to an end." She closed the door to the fitting room and turned to stare at herself in the mirror, a sad sigh escaping. Chip Ryder would never be her future, and Ryder Investments was always going to be the place where she climbed the corporate ladder just to sit at the top alone.

She pulled up to the shop that afternoon and parked her car behind Jackson's truck. She reached up to adjust the ponytail on top of her head and checked her makeup in the mirror. Once satisfied with her appearance, she climbed out of her car and walked confidently toward the main entrance. Feeling more comfortable in her steel-toed boots and khaki pants, her raglan t-shirt clung to her hips, giving her a relaxed vibe that she hadn't felt in days.

She stepped inside the garage and looked around. Dylan was standing in front of one of the cars, tinkering with something under the hood. Jackson was in the other corner, bent over the remnants of a motorcycle. He had removed his T-shirt and tucked it into the back of his jeans, and he had clearly been working for a few hours based on the slick sweat across his naked back. She swallowed heavily as she watched the thick muscles strain against each of his movements. He really was a good-looking man, she thought.

"Hey, Allison!" Dylan's voice announced her arrival, causing Jackson to look up and catch her gaze. Feeling a bit flustered, she nervously glanced around the garage, her hand trailing anxiously across the back of her neck.

"Hey, uh, sorry I'm late this afternoon. I had to do some shopping," she said, trying to regain her composure. When her eyes met Jackson's, he was looking at her with a small smirk.

"Nice threads. Must feel weird looking like us townsfolk," Jackson teased, and she cursed the fact that he did so in a convincing, friendly manner instead of his usual insulting tone.

She replied with a smile, "At least it's easier to walk in here when I'm not in heels."

"I'm sure those boots didn't cost twenty-five hundred dollars, either," he added with a grin. She narrowed her eyes at his joke while he walked toward her.

"Who would pay twenty-five hundred dollars for shoes?" Dylan chimed in before returning his attention to the car he was working on.

Jackson leaned in as he passed by her. "Yeah, who would do that, Allison?" She tried not to shiver as his lips passed over her ear, but her body betrayed her.

Following him as he headed toward the office, she closed the door behind her. He walked to the corner of the room and yanked a shirt off a hanger. As he pulled it over his head, her eyes were drawn to the small tattoo on his chest; a cluster of three circles overlapping. She averted her attention once he finished dressing and walked over to the desk. "So, uh, I got out my balance sheet and tried to open that program I'm supposed to put those numbers into, but the damn thing keeps beeping at me," Jackson explained to her, slipping his glasses onto his face.

He sat down at his computer and clicked the mouse on the screen, revealing a photo of a man and a woman making an obscene gesture. She chuckled, prompting him to explain. "Oh, that? That's my baby sister, Sam, and her boyfriend, Blake."

She shook her head in recognition, recalling Linda's conversation the other night at the diner. "Ah, Linda's kid."

"Oh, you must have met Blake's mom then," he said. "You spend enough time over at the diner, and she'll tell you their whole life story." As he clicked on another screen, the balance sheets popped up. "There we go." He pushed his glasses up onto the bridge of his nose and Allison couldn't help but stare again, because come on—she was still a woman.

He punched a few numbers into the fields, causing the computer to beep. "Okay, wait," she said as she reached out, placing her hand over his to still his movements. The moment their hands touched, she jerked hers back, feeling a surge of something she couldn't explain. "Sorry, you need to hit enter before you put the number in."

"What?" Clearing his throat, he sat up in his chair and leaned forward toward the screen.

"If you hit enter and then put in the numbers, it shouldn't beep," she clarified. Jackson followed her instructions and entered the numbers. This time, the computer accepted the entry.

"Well, I'll be damned. You're a goddamned miracle worker, Allison," he said with a loud laugh.

"It's an older program. They can be tricky," she said.

He started entering his data line by line. She tried not to find it endearing as she watched him. One finger poked the keys at each entry, biting his tongue as he concentrated on the screen. "So, by inputting each item, will that track all my expenses in one place?"

With a nod, she observed his focused gaze on the screen. His jaw tightened as he swallowed, and Allison found herself heating up in the confines of his small office. "Um, yes, that's the idea. It should also allow you to monitor your sales."

"Well, hot damn," he exclaimed, raising his voice and smacking the desk. "I've been held back by a simple enter key this whole time."

"In theory," she cautioned, "there's still more to learn."

"You must be a riot at parties, always killing the vibe," he said, his lips pursed. "Ever been told to lighten up?" She flinched, familiar with such comments. But was it really his place to point it out? "Hit a nerve, didn't I?"

Allison rolled her eyes. "You can't climb the corporate ladder *and* be the life of the party." She shrugged, thinking back to all the times she had excused herself early from the corporate office parties to finish off a proposal while everyone else enjoyed a cocktail or flirted with their administrative assistant.

"The corporate ladder is for ugly people and losers named Larry." Jackson wrinkled his face in disdain. She laughed at the comment. If only he knew how right he was.

"You're impossible. Anyone ever tell *you* that?" She chuckled, a genuine sound that had been absent for a while. He gazed at her with an unfamiliar expression. He blinked a few times, and Allison wasn't sure how to feel about the way he was staring.

"I, uh—I think we've learned enough for today. You wanna get out of here?" he asked.

"What? We only managed to stop your computer from beeping."

"I know, but I need to stretch my legs and walk Whiskey," he said, rising from his seat with a slight limp.

Looking down at her phone anxiously, she observed the text messages she had missed from Chip.

Chip

> Going to assume you didn't answer my phone call last night because you were doing your job

Chip

> Because otherwise I'm going to start to think you're ignoring me

Chip

> And you know how much I hate being ignored!!!

"You coming?" Jackson stood impatiently at the door, waiting for her.

Reluctantly, she sighed, not wanting to deal with Chip right now. "Fine, but no funny business this time."

"Darling, humor isn't one of my many talents," he said, winking at her as she followed him out of the office toward his truck.

Chapter Eleven

Jackson

J ax drove to the trail as the sun was setting beyond the trees, with Whiskey getting restless in the seat beside him. The dog bounced nervously back and forth between him and Allison, who was staring out the window as the car pulled off the main road. She had seemed distant since leaving the garage, almost as if she had something weighing on her mind.

Jax watched her for longer than was appropriate. Without the heels and suit, Allison almost seemed like a different person. More relaxed and less uptight. It was apparent that something in her demeanor had shifted.

He couldn't help but notice, with her hair pulled into a ponytail, that she had a strawberry-shaped birthmark nestled behind her right ear. The length of time he spent staring at her made him feel like a stalker. He blamed Whiskey for spending so much time climbing into her lap. He rationalized that keeping tabs on his dog was simply good ownership.

Still, if he allowed himself a moment of honesty, there was something quite attractive about her today, even if it might literally kill him to admit it.

Jax parked the truck and climbed out, whistling for Whiskey to follow him. "I figured we could walk down to the bridge." He pointed toward a path leading off into a wooded section of trees. "Whiskey enjoys chasing the squirrels in the area."

"Then by all means, let's take your dog to harass some poor small creatures," she said, blowing a piece of her hair away from her face as she stared off into the woods.

"It's all in good fun," he said, patting his dog's head as Whiskey jumped around happily at his feet. "Ain't that right, boy!" Whiskey took off down the trail they had frequented so often since his accident, barking playfully and hopping around in patches of grass as if he were still a young pup. Allison soon caught up to him, walking slowly by his side as Jax pushed through the slight discomfort in his knee.

There were times his injury didn't bother him much; the aches and pains were simply another part of his life. But on days like today, when he was out hiking a trail with a young woman beside him, well, those were the days when he should feel more like a strapping, young, thirty-one-year-old man and less like a grumpy old codger who needed a walking stick just to take five steps. At this rate, he was six months away from yelling at a few of the neighborhood kids to 'stay off his lawn.'

Not that he was trying to impress Allison. At least, that was what he was trying to convince himself of when he angrily stepped down and cursed as his knee gave out once again. He mumbled incoherently after the curse slipped out more forcefully than he intended.

"What happened?" She looked at him with those sympathetic eyes, the ones that made him feel like a pathetic invalid again, and he quickly recovered his steps.

"Nothing, just stepped down wrong. I'm fine," he reassured, in a cold and dismissive tone. Allison seemed to study him as if she was looking for a reason to counter his claim. He grumbled and followed his dog down the trail. "So, uh, tell me Allison, what made you decide to get into the exciting world of real estate and finance? Were all the really fun jobs already taken?" he asked.

"I'll have you know my job is quite exciting." She laughed. "It is highly competitive, very rewarding, and on most days ... alright, I suppose on most days it can be quite boring."

"That's what I thought," he said with a scoff. "You office types lack sunshine and fresh air."

"I do go outside, Jackson. My job requires me to travel often, actually."

He teased playfully, "Travel to where? Other offices?"

The snort was unladylike, and she glanced away. "Sometimes, but there are times I go to job sites or out of town to review properties."

A small growl left his throat. "Like my shop..."

"I came out here last year to survey your property when your dad was trying to sell the business. My investment firm was very interested in purchasing it from your father."

He hadn't realized she had been the one to come to Titusville last year, or that she had been inside his shop before he met her. "What's with the hard-on for Lancaster's? What interest could you possibly have in some Podunk town's auto shop?"

She shook her head and slowed her steps. "In case you haven't noticed, you don't exactly have any competition in town."

"So, what you're telling me is that I *could* be very profitable if only I wasn't *so* stupid." She walked ahead of him, and he tried not to stare at the back of her neck, where the strawberry mark lived. Damn, if he didn't love strawberries.

She turned around and faced him with a frown on her face. "I never said you were stupid. And if I recall, you said you aren't either. You just lack the business acumen needed to really be successful."

"Wow, acumen. Big word, city slicker, have you been saving that one for me this whole time?"

She sighed and chewed on her bottom lip, turning back around as she picked up the pace toward Whiskey on the other end of the trail. "Are you always this combative, or do you just save it for me?" She looked back at him over her shoulder, teasing him with a smile that was more devilish than he was prepared for. Smirking, he caught up to her just as they made it to the small bridge.

Whiskey, ahead of them, chased a nearby squirrel and disappeared under the bridge. The gentle sound of his bark echoed in the canopy of trees above them.

The sun was setting off in the distance, casting rays of light across the creek, illuminating the water beneath the bridge. He could see a small twinkle in the distance blinking in and out along the creek bed. "What is that?" Allison asked, staring off into the distance.

Jax grumbled, "Oh, come on, please don't tell me you've never seen a firefly?" She stared at the blinking lights. "All this time, I've been calling you that name. Even a city slicker has to know what they are?"

"I know what a firefly is. I just don't see them in the city often. And honestly, I've gotten used to men calling me derogatory names, so I've learned to ignore what they call me most of the time." She shrugged.

"It wasn't a derogatory term, though." He paused, suddenly feeling like an ass. "Honestly, it's the hair. It damn near glowed the first time I saw you. It was the first thing that came to mind."

Almost subconsciously, she reached up and touched her hair, responding with a simple, "Oh."

"I can stop if it bothers you," he said, turning to lean against the bridge and look down into the water.

"It's fine." She glanced back into the woods and smiled at the glowing bugs. "I've never seen so many in one place."

"There are a lot of things you can see out here that you can't see in the city." Leaning over, he focused his attention on the creek, where Whiskey was joyfully jumping in and out of the water below.

He glanced over at Allison as the light cast across her face, illuminating her in a soft glow. His attraction to her irritated him. She was annoying and difficult, and yet he couldn't stop staring at her. He had been counting down the time until she left town. And now...

She squealed, dislodging him from his thoughts. "Should he be doing that?" He followed her gaze to the creek as Whiskey jumped backward, revealing something lodged in his mouth. The dog growled and shook his head, water squirting out from his fur and mouth.

"Whiskey, put it down!" he hollered, rushing off the bridge toward the stream of water below. He could hear Allison yelling behind him, and he growled in her direction, "Stay there." The last thing he needed was her trying to stumble around on the rocky path down here in the dark.

When he reached his dog, he found a small squirrel hanging from its mouth, squirming and fighting against his jaw. Whiskey yelped and backed away as he approached. "Put him down, boy. We only chase them, we don't catch." The pup danced at his feet the moment he released the animal, and the squirrel shuffled off into the trees. Jax bent down, his knee cracking, and checked the dog's mouth to ensure there was no bleeding. "Damn, boy, what were you thinking?"

"Is he alright?" Allison's voice sounded behind him, causing him to groan.

He closed his eyes and exhaled. "I told you to stay up there."

"Did he eat it?" Her voice sounded terrified.

"Did he eat it?" Annoyed, he groaned and turned toward her, his hip aching painfully as he twisted. "He was just trying to play with it."

"By chewing on a defenseless animal?" She shrilled so loudly it caused Whiskey to jump backward and whine while tucking his tail underneath him. Jax stood up and patted Whiskey on his head to calm him down. "Are you rewarding him for almost eating a squirrel?"

He muttered, "Would you stop being a bleeding heart? All this screeching is scaring him."

"Bleeding heart!" Her voice got even louder as she scoffed and turned away from him, repeating angrily, "Bleeding heart," before storming off the rocky pathway. Just as she was about to leave, she screamed. There was a splash, and he turned around just in time to see her foot slip off the rocky embankment, tumbling into the creek water under the bridge.

Whiskey galloped toward her, his tail swishing behind him.

Jax raced toward her, sloshing into the creek water toward the redhead who was lying face down in the bubbling creek bed. His heart raced as he reached her and grabbed her by the shoulder, pulling her out of the water as her mouth opened wide and she gulped for air. Breathing a sigh of relief and pinching his eyes shut, he tried to slow his heart before sitting her up and pulling her into his arms. "Are you alright?" he asked, pressing his hands to her neck and shoulders, his eyes darting back and forth as he glanced at her face.

She stared at him, slack jawed, as if she was in shock. "I—I don't know?"

"Does anything hurt?" he asked. She shook her head slowly in a daze as his fingers pressed against the back of her neck. "Allison..." he asked, desperate for her to respond and let him know she was fine.

She blinked slowly, looking at him, her red hair stuck to the sides of her face and forehead. "I—" She swallowed, blinked again, and then closed her eyes.

Jax felt like his heart was going to beat out of his chest. "Allison, open your eyes. Tell me what hurts."

Her eyes opened a fraction of an inch, and she shook her head. "I'm fine, I think." Her wet lips were shining in the moonlight as she bit down on her bottom lip.

"What the hell were you thinking? I told you not to come down here!" His voice raised over the bubbling creek. "You could have gotten hurt or—hell, why can't you just listen for once?" She was staring at him silently, blinking at him with those blue eyes that he could hardly see in the darkness, and her wet lips, those haunting wet lips, glistening in the moonlight as she sat shivering in the creek. Dammit, Jax was just so damn angry at her.

Because Allison Hanover was such a pain in the ass.

A pain in the ass who had no right to be staring at him like that with those blue eyes and those wet lips.

It was irrational and probably the dumbest thing he had ever done, but before he could stop and think about it, he pressed his mouth to those wet lips. He pulled her into his arms, her soaking body pressed against him, and placed his lips exactly where he swore he would never touch her. It was a kiss like nothing he had ever experienced before because, goddamn if that woman didn't kiss like a siren. She might have been stunned momentarily by his mouth touching hers, but it didn't take long before he felt her lips against his, and the heat of her tongue pressing into his mouth.

He wasn't sure who moaned. Hell, it was probably him, because the kiss was that damn good. Her mouth was warm and wet from the creek, but her lips slid against his with ease. He swallowed every moan that hummed from her throat, pulling her soaking body firmly against his chest. His hands slid firmly behind her neck, fingers massaging that spot, that delicious spot with the strawberry mark. His tongue glided along her jaw to get a taste of her and the moment he licked her salty skin, she made a sound so sinful he felt his entire body light on fire.

However, the sound brought his world to a screeching halt. Before he knew what was happening, he was falling backward. The frigid creek water dousing the burning fire that just seconds before was threatening to set them both ablaze. "What the hell?" he growled as he looked up and saw her shadow hovering over him.

A splash of water hit him in the face as she stalked out of the water, holding onto Whiskey's fur. "I want to go back to my hotel," she said, climbing toward the bridge.

Dragging himself out of the creek, he sloshed up toward the trail where Allison was standing with her arms crossed against her chest. "Warn a guy next time you want to go from hot to cold like that," he said.

"No one asked you to kiss me," she said angrily, tilting her chin away from him.

He chuckled. "Yeah, you seemed real disgusted back there, city girl." With a grunt, he started walking back toward the truck. "Come on, let's get you back before you turn into a country toad or something awful." Without looking back and ignoring the pain in his knee, he angrily stormed back the way they came, leaving Allison to trail slowly behind him.

Chapter Twelve

Allison

Allison was sitting in the corner booth at Linda's Diner, staring out the window as her plate of eggs and avocado toast got cold on the table in front of her as the sun rose on Tuesday morning.

Jackson Lancaster had kissed her.

She was uncertain about what upset her more—the fact that he had kissed her or that she hadn't immediately pushed him away.

She tried to act indignant, pretending to be furious that he had dared to kiss her without an invitation. She hadn't leaned in or closed her eyes. Surely, she had shown no interest in him. In fact, they were always at each other's throats. Yet, when he kissed her, she didn't pull back or show disgust. Instead, Allison had kissed him back, which puzzled and infuriated her.

Why did she kiss Jackson Lancaster?

To make matters worse, she was certain that she was the one who deepened the kiss by moving her tongue into his mouth. Frustrated by the memory, she audibly groaned and closed her eyes, her cheeks warming at the thought of his lips on hers, his tongue trailing along her jaw. She hadn't expected him to be such a good kisser—or, hell, maybe she had, which was why she had been so determined not to kiss him in the first place.

She looked back at her plate, violently stabbing her eggs. Damn Jackson and his soft lips!

Linda's voice broke in, interrupting her scandalous thoughts. "Anything else I can get you, dear?" Allison glanced up to see Linda's concerned expression as she rubbed her hands together.

"Oh, um. No, I'm fine," Allison said, shaking her head and returning her gaze to her plate.

The woman laughed. "Based on the state of those eggs, I'm uncertain that's entirely true."

Surveying the mess on her plate, Allison sighed—it resembled a crime scene, a sunny side up murder, with her as the prime suspect. "Ugh," she muttered, dropping her fork onto her plate. "Sorry, I guess I'm just distracted."

Linda's smile put Allison at ease. "Well, if there is one thing my kids tell me, it's that I'm a good listener."

"You have more than just the kid in New York?"

Linda gestured toward the empty seat across from her, seeking permission to join Allison, who nodded in approval. Linda settled into the booth. "My daughter, Kelley, moved to California last year. She's in the nursing program at Berkeley."

"Oh, that's amazing. My dad works at UPMC in Erie," Allison mentioned casually. "Medicine has been in my family since I was born."

Linda chuckled. "I actually asked Ken about you. I didn't realize you were Stacy's kid."

The mention of her mother surprised her. "You know my mom?"

"Oh, honey, you can't grow up around here without knowing everyone who was born in Titusville," she said, searching her pockets and pulling out her wallet. "I was hoping to show you this. It's an old photo from high school I found." She slid it across the table. "That's your mom, and that's me," she said, pointing to the two faces in a trio of young girls. She recognized her mother immediately. She was always fascinated by how much she resembled her mom. Between Linda and her mother stood a third woman, with a soft smile on her face. Allison recognized her as Ken's wife, Mary. "That's Jackson's mom. The three of us were very good friends. Hard not to be in a town this size."

"I don't really know much about their life before they left Titusville. I didn't even know Ken until he called last year to sell his shop," she admitted.

"Ken told me the entire story when we talked last week," Linda said. Allison shouldn't have been surprised; after all, small towns were known for sharing their gossip. "So, how are things going with

Jackson? I thought you were only going to be around for a day or two?"

Allison swore she tried to keep her facial expression neutral, but she must have flinched or rolled her eyes, as the woman caught something in the way she reacted and immediately made a humming sound. "It's been..." she exhaled, sinking slightly into the booth, "difficult."

Linda frowned. "You know, last year was hard for the whole Lancaster family. Sam came home after being gone for a long absence and, well, that caused a lot of turmoil between my son and his best friend, Dylan. And Jackson, well God bless that boy after everything he went through with his accident." Allison narrowed her eyes. "And I'm not giving him any excuses. I know how he can be. Stubborn as a mule. Trust me, I've babysat both those boys over the years, and I've seen the trouble they get up to. But you won't find anyone as loyal or hardworking."

"I don't think he trusts that I have good intentions in helping him," she sighed.

Linda stared at her like she was looking right through her. It was the first time Allison felt slightly uncomfortable in the conversation. "Well, do you?" She paused. "Have good intentions?"

Guilt slipped into her mind as she thought about the goal Chip had given her to get Jax to sell his shop, a goal she didn't really give a crap about honestly. "He's so determined not to listen to what I have to tell him because I come from the city that I fear it doesn't matter in the long run if I have good intentions or not."

The woman appeared to be sizing her up, as if she could see through her and knew Allison was here with an ulterior motive. She squirmed in her chair, guilt eating at her as she tried to make herself smaller. The woman finally spoke. "If he gives you any more trouble, tell that boy I'll turn him over my knee."

Allison laughed. "He's over thirty years old. He's hardly a child anymore, Linda."

She stared at her with a cheeky grin. "I've changed that boy's diaper. He'll always be a kid to me."

Allison approached the garage an hour later and parked behind Jackson's truck. She switched off her car just as her phone rang. Glancing at the screen, she noticed Chip's name. She wasn't in the mood to deal with her boss that morning, but she also realized she had been ghosting him for too long and he must have already taken notice.

Reluctantly she answered his call. "Hey, Chip."

"So, your phone does work?" His voice carried a hint of annoyance, clarifying to her that this conversation wouldn't be pleasant.

"I've been busy, Chip."

"Being busy doesn't excuse you from checking in. You know how crucial this is to me," he said, his breath heavy in her ear.

"I understand, and I warned you not to get your hopes up. This guy will not sell to us," she said. She was tiring of his ridiculous quest for Jackson's shop. Allison didn't know how many other ways to tell him it wasn't going to happen.

He chuckled. "And I instructed you to change his mind. What dirt do you have on him? Any weaknesses we can exploit? Drinking problems? Health issues from his accident? Secret love child?" She closed her eyes, leaning back in her seat as he bombarded her with questions. Unfortunately, he wasn't giving up on this. "Are you listening, Allie Cat?"

"Yes, Chip! I hear you!" she shouted.

"Are you sure? Because all I'm hearing is attitude and I'm looking for solutions," he said.

She closed her eyes and rubbed her temples. "I'll work on something today." She sighed, figuring she could just go back to the hotel and half ass some stupid report on the shop that would never go anywhere.

"I expect results soon, Allie Cat. Otherwise, you'll be reporting to Larry when you return." Before she could respond, the call ended abruptly. Frustrated, she let out a scream, hitting the steering wheel as she tried to compose herself. Surely, he would never let Larry take over her accounts. Larry couldn't even figure out how to run his data analytics dashboard without crashing his computer and calling her to bail him out.

Staring down at her broken nails, she knew deep down that he wasn't bluffing, which was even more frustrating. Life was cruel, and fairness was a fantasy.

Once she felt she could face other people without cursing loudly, she exited the vehicle and walked into the garage. The first thing she noticed was that the music was different. Gone was the loud hair metal band music that Jackson always played. Today, it was replaced by the soothing guitar sounds of Noah Kahan's "Stick Season," playing on the radio.

She looked around the empty garage until she heard a clank and stepped toward the sound, finding a pair of feet sticking out from underneath a lifted Honda. "Hello?" she announced as Dylan slid out from under the car and looked up at her.

"Oh, hey, sorry, didn't hear anyone come in," he said. "Jax isn't here."

"Oh!" She was surprised, suddenly feeling exposed as she stood in the middle of the garage.

"Yeah, said something 'bout needing to take care of stuff, but I have no idea what that *stuff* might be." Dylan shrugged. Allison looked around nervously, realizing it must mean she wasn't the only one upset about last night's incident. When she turned back toward Dylan, he was staring at her with suspicion. "Come to think of it, he's been acting like an ass since he came home yesterday. Something happen last night with you two?"

She chuckled and stared at her feet. "Weird. I thought that was the usual way he acted. Not sure how you tell the difference."

"I think I know my brother, Miss, and Jax might act like a jerk sometimes, but he's not actually an asshole," Dylan said with such emphasis that her eyes jerked up to meet his. He was staring at her, tapping a screwdriver against his palm.

Allison lowered her eyes and sighed. "Yeah, well, I'm not your brother's keeper, so I have no idea what his problem is." Glancing around the garage, she noticed a line of cars outside waiting to be serviced. "Looks like you guys are busy today."

"We're always busy," Dylan said with an air of attitude. "I'll probably die under the hood of a Chevy," he grumbled as he lay back down on the creeper and slid under the car.

"Isn't that a Honda?" she said, directing her voice toward the ground so he could hear her.

He slid back out, staring up at her. "What?"

She pointed at the car he was under. "Aren't you under a Honda?"

He smiled and chuckled. "I didn't plan to die today."

"Oh, right." She laughed. "I mean, that's probably smart."

He pointed to the toolbox behind her. "I don't mean to be like my brother, but can you grab me that Phillips head?" She stared at the red box and frowned. "It's the screwdriver that looks like an x on the bottom, not the flat one." Stepping over to the box, she searched for the tool he described and handed it confidently to him. "Thanks."

"Why can't they just call the tools by names that make sense?" She leaned against the car, trying to work out a better name for the tool as he slipped underneath it again. "Cross thingy," she mumbled softly.

She heard the sound of metal on metal as he worked on the vehicle. "Beats me. I've been using these things since I could walk. I guess I just never questioned it." She watched as his legs kicked slightly, and then he pushed out from under the car, sitting up and brushing his hands on his pants.

"I gotta ask," he began as he stood up. "Why are you still here, Allison?"

She felt her cheeks flush hot as she pushed off the car, stammering, "Oh, I, uh, I'm sorry. I didn't mean to disturb you. I ... I... can go."

"No, that's not what I—I meant here, in Titusville. Why are you still here, in town?" he clarified, leaving her even more dumbfounded.

"Well, I'm teaching Jackson how to—" she started before he was interrupting her.

"That's bullshit and you know it." He shrugged, tossing his tool back into the toolbox. "My brother isn't exactly your star pupil."

She sighed. "Your father was very persistent, and Jackson seems very adamant that he wants to keep his business."

Dylan cleaned his hands with a rag while listening to her. "He will never sell this place, *just so you're aware*." He seemed to emphasize the end of his sentence to make himself clear.

"I ... I know that," she quickly stuttered out. "He seems very passionate about that fact."

"Jax started working here when he was just a kid, before our mom died. I remember she would make sandwiches and bring them up here for my dad and Jax to eat for lunch. I was always jealous because it meant that the two of them got to spend all this time together, alone." Dylan hopped up onto the counter, taking a seat and examining the clipboard of tasks for the day. He chuckled.

"If I'd known it meant they were doing all this manual labor, I might not have asked to be included so much."

She glanced at the motorcycle, still in pieces in the shop's corner. "How come that one never gets finished? Isn't the client going to get tired of waiting?"

Dylan looked up, following her gaze, and scoffed. "I don't think the owner is ready to finish it, otherwise it would be done." Seeing her confusion, he clarified. "The bike belongs to Jax."

Suddenly, things made more sense. "How long has he been building it?" she asked.

He didn't bother to look up from his clipboard. "Soon as he could get around without that damn walker." She could hardly imagine Jackson with a walker. Just the irritation it must have caused him alone almost made her laugh out loud. "I don't know if he's afraid to finish it because it means he has to get back on it again, or because he's afraid he can't." He tossed the clipboard back onto the counter and jumped down.

She stared at the bike, the pieces strewn about the corner of the garage, and tried not to think about what was stopping Jackson from finishing his bike. It wasn't her problem, anyway.

"So, you really didn't answer my question," Dylan responded again. "I get my dad is persistent, but he's not even here. Just tell him to fuck off and go home if Jax is such an ass. Why keep coming back here and putting up with his shit?" He stared up at the ceiling and then exhaled. "I'm sure you make a solid paycheck back in the city, probably way more than you need to not have to deal with us small-town losers just because some old guy asked you to do him a favor."

"It's not about money." Alright, Allison, it wasn't *all* about money, she thought. "Our parents were friends growing up and I'm not just going to tell him I can't help."

"I would," he grumbled. "Somehow I think you would too. I don't exactly buy this selfless in-it-for-nothing reason for you being here." He stared at her with a frown, and Allison felt like if anyone might catch on to her, it was Dylan. Plus, she didn't really know what was keeping her here. She didn't really care about Chip's interest in the shop, even though he was pissing her off by threatening her job if she didn't at least attempt to make a play for it. "I don't know why you're so interested in Jackson or our shop, but I don't think you're doing it out of the kindness of your heart. And honestly, I'd rather you just go back to Erie and let Jackson continue to one finger poke his keyboard while we try to figure out how to do this on our own instead of watching my big brother get swindled by some city girl with ulterior motives."

She felt as if he had slapped her in the face. Not that he was entirely wrong. Even if she wasn't actively trying to get him to sell the shop to Chip, her boss had sent her here with those motives. And if Jackson sold his shop, it *would* benefit her firm, even if she didn't care if he sold it or not. But it also wasn't like she was trying to help Jackson, because it would actually benefit him. Did she actually care if Jackson's shop went under if he didn't learn how to manage his business?

She blinked and bit her lip, pondering how to reply. "Look, Dylan," she began, but he cut her off.

"Save it," he said. "My brother might be open to hearing your pitch, but I'm not interested. You either show him what he needs to see or leave. It's that simple. If he's not receptive, that's his issue, not yours. Either way, I suggest you move on quickly. My brother has been through a lot this past year, and I'm not going to sit back and watch him get hurt again."

With that, he turned his back on her and walked away, leaving her standing alone in the middle of the garage.

Chapter Thirteen

Jackson

Jackson's chair squeaked as it rocked back and forth along the wooden porch slats of his cabin, his beer bottle slipping against his lips as he let the liquor glide down his throat. He had spent the better part of his day drowning his feelings and pouting on his porch chair, thinking it was a good plan when he woke up and skipped work on a Tuesday. However, now he realized it was after 7:00 PM, and he was drunk and starving, with a fridge full of nothing but beer and salami. Perhaps he might have made an error in his plans.

Luckily for him, he could call in an order for dinner at Linda's Diner. It helped that his sister was intimately familiar with the owner's son, and Linda had a sweet spot for him, so she offered to have his order dropped off at his place within the hour.

His phone buzzed on the table beside him, with a message from his father.

> Hey son, just checking in to see how things are going with Allison.

Jax frowned, shaking his head, unsure of how to respond to his father.

She's a pain in the ass. Oh, and no big deal, but I kissed her!

Jax figured that might bring about more questions than he was prepared to answer, so he kept it short and simple.

A pair of headlights flashed across his face as the car headed down the main driveway and slipped past the house toward his cabin on the back lot. His stomach grumbled at the thought of a nice juicy burger and fries. The headlights flashed off, leaving only the glow of the porch light above him, and someone stepped out of the car. He squinted as the woman came into view. "Someone order a burger and fries?"

"Well, damn," he sighed, setting his beer on the small table beside him. "What the hell are you doing here, Allison?"

"I was eating at the diner tonight, and Linda asked if I could drop off a special order," she said with an anxious smile.

He stared at her face, examining the way her eyes sparkled the moment she smiled, the way her nose crinkled as she bit her lip. But he found himself stuck once he got to her lips, unable to glance away. Just twenty-four hours ago, he had kissed those lips, and he hadn't been able to stop thinking about them since.

"Why would she send you?" he asked, snapping his eyes away from her lips.

She shrugged and handed him the food. "You know Linda better than I do."

Chuckling, he relaxed into his rocking chair. "Yeah, yeah I do."

"Nice place you got back here, Grandpa," she teased, leaning against the railing of his porch.

"Oh, you have all the jokes tonight, Firefly." He laughed. "I'm sure you city folk don't have the faintest idea what quaint and homey mean, anyway."

"I know what it means. My apartment is very homey."

He laughed out loud. "And what does homey mean to you?"

Watching her think about it, he observed her staring off into the distance of the wooded area beside his cabin. "My apartment overlooks downtown Erie."

"Oh yes, traffic is very homey," he interrupted with a snort.

"Okay smartass, I wasn't finished." Her sarcastic response had him tingling in his inebriated state. He gestured for her to continue speaking. "I wake up in the morning, and I can look down on the city and simply watch as the world moves on without any-one realizing that I'm observing them."

"So, you're a voyeur?" He playfully lifted his brow and winked. "Like to watch, eh?"

"How many of those have you had tonight?" she asked, ges-turing toward the empty bottle at his feet.

He finished the beer in his hand and stood up. "Enough to make me interesting." He paused in front of her. "You want to stick around, maybe knock back a cold one?" he asked. "Or are you too afraid I'll kiss you again?"

Without even flinching, she straightened up and stared into his eyes. "I don't scare that easily, Jackson," she said with a fire behind her words that intrigued him.

He exhaled through his nose, his brow furrowing. "I'll get you a beer then, Allison," he said with a playful raise of his brow.

Stepping into the house, he stood in front of his fridge, staring at the contents, or lack thereof, before reaching in and grabbing a couple of beers. It seemed like a stupid idea to offer her one, especially given his current state—half drunk and full of feelings. He probably should have just sent her back on the road.

However, something in her eyes tonight told him she wanted him to ask her to stay. It might have been the alcohol, but regardless, his fool mouth ended up telling her to stick around, so the damage was already done.

Walking back out onto the porch, he noticed she had moved to the swing, her knees pulled up under her chin as she glided softly against the night breeze. Twisting the bottle cap off her beer, he handed it to her. "I'm surprised you don't drink out of cans."

Staring aghast, he sat down on his rocker. "I'm not a savage." Her light chuckle made him look up, the twinkle in her eyes catching just right under the porch light as she sipped the beer. She scrunched her nose in disgust as the liquid went down. He couldn't help but laugh. "Not a beer drinker either, eh?"

"Not a drinker," she said. "It takes a bit to get used to."

"Yeah, nothing like drinking a bottle of piss water," he said, looking appreciatively at his beer, a smile playing across his lips. "It's an acquired taste."

She sputtered out a cough and placed the bottle in her lap. "I'll take your word for it." They sat in silence for a moment, and Jax took a bite of his hamburger before his stomach started growling at him again. "So, I stopped by the shop today." He swallowed his food slowly as she continued speaking. "Dylan said you didn't come in."

"Yeah, I took a personal day," he said.

She nodded. "I see. Look, Jackson, if it had anything to do with what happened at the creek—"

"It was personal," he interrupted in a firm tone.

They sat in a silence that drifted into an almost uncomfortable territory. "Dylan told me that the bike you are always building is yours."

Damn, maybe they could go back to sitting in silence. "Dylan has a big mouth."

Allison sighed, sat up on the swing, and braced her feet on the ground as she glared at him. "I'm just trying to make conversation with you. Are you going to be grumpy the whole time, or should I just go?"

Closing his eyes, he exhaled through his mouth and leaned back in his chair. "Beer makes me moody."

"Do you inject it through an IV daily? Is that your excuse?" she asked.

Jax peered through partially opened lids as the corner of his lip upturned. "Alright, fair play, Allison."

He contemplated a further response, glancing down at his shoes. Something about her presence unsettled him. She made him feel uneasy and uncertain. Allison was confident, smart, so sure of herself, and Jackson was none of those things. "I'm sure you're probably gonna tell me the bike is a drain on my revenue," he said with a smirk. "Though I paid for the parts out of my personal funds, I do work on it on company time when I don't have other jobs to do."

She stared at him. "I'm not here to give you a finance lesson, Jackson."

"Yeah, well, I should probably just donate the damn thing, anyway." With a shrug, he brought the beer bottle to his mouth and drank, the alcohol tasting stale and warm. The conversation was getting to him. "I'm probably never gonna to ride again, anyway."

"Did the doctors tell you that you couldn't?" she asked.

His shrug felt like a childish gesture, reminiscent of the kind he used to give his mother growing up when she would ask him if he would watch his sister when he wanted to play with his friends instead. "Not in those words, no. I've built up the strength in my legs so I can keep it upright, but I need an electric start now, cuz the kick-start is a bitch." Admitting this crap pissed him off. It made him feel smaller somehow. Less of a man. And Jackson Lancaster was a warm-blooded man.

"I'm sure you'll be back on a bike before you know it," she reassured. But how the hell could she know that? She wasn't even here for the accident. She didn't know what he had been through to even get to his current state. Instead of a reply, he simply grumbled incoherently. Allison was at least receptive enough to take that as a cue to drop the topic, pivoting to something new. "Is there a reason you don't live in the main house?"

She was just full of annoying questions tonight. "Is there something wrong with my house?"

"No, not at all," she quickly added. "I just assumed the big house was empty."

"Dylan lives in an apartment above the garage that my parents built for him." He gestured toward the house. "Dad hasn't been back since he went on his grand tour of the country, but when he returns, the place belongs to him." Pointing to his cabin behind him, he added, "This one's mine."

"So, you're planning to live in this small cabin forever?" she asked.

"That was the idea," he said, taking another sip of his beer.

She looked around, examining his cabin, and he was about to ask her if she was the goddamn IRS or something when she spoke. "What about having a family or a wife? Seems a bit cramped."

"You filling out an application?" he teased with a smirk, making her shrink back in her seat. "Because, in case you didn't notice, I have no prospects. No plans for marriage or kids."

"You don't want kids?" she asked, a look of surprise he didn't expect flashed across her face.

He raised an eyebrow suspiciously. "Is this an interrogation?"

She chuckled softly, taking a sip of her beer with a smile. "I was just curious, that's all."

"I never said I didn't want kids. But, as you can see, I've lived here my whole life and haven't found the right woman to have kids with. And that's sure as hell not going to change anytime soon." He winked, adding, "Unless you're volunteering."

She shot him a glare and glanced at the ceiling. "You don't even like me."

"Doesn't mean it wouldn't be fun," he said with a playful smirk. Suddenly, the small pillow from his porch swing flew toward him. He caught it with both hands, playfully throwing it back at her, causing her to squeal.

"You're an idiot!" she screeched, but he couldn't ignore the fact that she was still smiling.

Allison Hanover looked really pretty when she smiled.

Taking another sip of his beer, he gazed out into the darkened woods. "My folks built this place after they got married," he confessed, unsure why he was sharing so much. He'd blame his over sharing on the excessive amount of alcohol in the morning. "Dad always wanted to travel, but he had to tend to the shop, and Mom wanted a place where they could escape. I guess I enjoy knowing that this place meant something to them."

Leaning back on the swing, Allison pursed her lips together and let out a soft whistle. "Wow, who would have thought with that prickly exterior that there was this gooey sentimental softy hidden in there?"

"Don't you dare let that get out," he warned playfully. "I'll deny it."

"I'm not sure that people would believe you. Everyone I talk to seems to think you're some big teddy bear," she said, trying to hold back her laughter.

Jax blinked and then shook his head. "You need to stop talking to the people in this town. Liars, the lot of them," he joked, feeling the effects of too many beers without having eaten enough food.

Looking at Allison, who was gazing at him, he felt a shift in the air, like something had changed and he was too slow to catch up. "I should go," she said suddenly, standing up.

Jax's mind raced to catch up. He set his beer down and stood up. He caught her by the arm before she got to the bottom of the porch steps. "Allison..." She looked up, almost surprised to hear her name, but not as surprised as he was to say it. Unsure of why he had stopped her, he struggled to find the right words for the moment.

"Jackson, I should..." She paused, taking a soft breath before... "Ah, to hell with it." With that, she reached behind his neck and pulled him toward her, causing him to stumble forward as their lips met in a forceful kiss. Surprised by her boldness, he held onto her hips, reciprocating with a passion he couldn't quite comprehend.

The kiss by the creek had been born out of emotion, a surge of relief upon realizing she was safe. It had been unexpected and unplanned. But this kiss, initiated by her, was something entirely different.

The kiss was needy and desperate. Her lips pressed urgently against him, as if unable to get enough of him. It ignited every nerve in him, sending a fire through his body.

His fingers brushed against the edge of her shirt, revealing a glimpse of her silky skin. She was softer than anything his calloused hands had ever touched before. Flattening his palms against her warm flesh, he heard her moan into his mouth, and his heart raced from the sound alone.

This woman was gasoline, and he was willing to set himself on fire just to feel the way she burned.

Her delicate fingers played with his hair while her nails lightly scratched behind his ears. A moan escaped him as her tongue grazed his chin. Gripping her hips, he pulled her closer, the porch against his back. This woman drove him crazy in so many ways, but right now, he couldn't get enough of her.

He had dreamed of making her angry, listening to how loud she could yell while driving her out of town, but now he could only think about driving into the soft spot between her legs while she screamed his name.

As his hand moved down her back, he caressed her firm behind, feeling her nails tighten in his hair. He was imagining all the ways he could get her out of her clothing when she suddenly pulled away, panting, with darkened eyes fixed on him. Her hands slid down his chest as she teasingly admitted, "You were right, that was fun." She walked away, leaving him with a playful smile and a clear view of his arousal.

"Hey, you're just gonna leave me like this?" He gestured toward his obvious hard on.

She looked back with a smile, biting her lip. "You hurt your leg, not your wrist. I think you can take care of that on your own." Her tongue darted out to lick the top of her teeth before she turned around and climbed into her car.

Allison Hanover might be pretty to look at when she smiled, but she was damn lethal when you watched her walk away.

Chapter Fourteen

Allison

Hot fingers fluttered across Allison's stomach, leaving a trail of fire until they reached her collarbone, making every nerve in her body feel as if lightning bolts were tap dancing just under her skin. The man's mouth was hot and wet, his tongue sliding across her jaw until it reached just below her earlobe, where she could feel the prickle of hot breath on her ear. His lips moved slowly as he spoke. "Light up for me, Firefly." Trembling, sweat soaking her skin, she cried out, "Jackson!"

Suddenly jolting awake in bed, she gasped for air, her chest rising and falling rapidly.

With the sudden realization that she was still at the bed-and-breakfast, she closed her eyes and sank back into her covers. Apparently, she was dreaming about Jackson now. That was a recent development. Which was just wonderful, she thought sarcastically.

Kissing him last night seemed foolish, but his openness and the way he spoke had stirred something in her. Maybe it was just desire, but he had looked incredibly attractive last night. When he stopped her before she left, calling her by her name, not a nickname, something inside her snapped, and she craved to kiss him.

Damn, if Jackson Lancaster wasn't the best kisser she had ever laid lips on. It took everything in her to get in her car last night and drive home instead of dragging him inside of his cabin to let him do whatever he wanted to her. Despite his injuries, she knew he was capable of things beyond her imagination.

Since their time at the creek, she had done a lot of imagining.

Tossing the covers off, she rolled out of the bed and begrudgingly got ready for a *cold* shower.

Mrs. Hattie appeared anxious as Allison entered the small living room that Wednesday morning, holding the register book in her lap while looking forlornly out the window.

"Everything alright this morning?"

The woman jumped, the sudden sound echoing through the room. "Oh dear, you scared me," she said, placing a hand over her heart.

Allison walked toward her, glancing at the book in her lap, recognizing it to have bank balances on each line. "Are you sure you're alright?"

The old woman sighed and closed the book. "Things just aren't like they used to be," she said. "It's so hard to run a business when you only have one client." The woman laughed sadly and reached out to touch Allison's hand. "Nothing for you to worry about, dear."

"Anything I can help with. After all, I am an analyst."

"Oh, I would never take advantage of you like that." She laughed. "You're my guest. My problems are not your problems, sweetie." She stood up and placed the book in the drawer and straightened her shirt. "Now, how are things going with our Jackson?" Allison felt her face flush as she looked away. "Oh, I see you've made some progress."

"Mrs. Hattie!" she scolded the woman. "Jackson is—well, it's complicated."

"Oh, it always is." She grinned, the lines of amusement crinkling around her eyes. "But then, matters of the heart always are."

"Jackson and I are working together on a purely professional basis. I'm here to help him with his shop, that's all," she stated firmly, unsure if she was trying to convince herself or Mrs. Hattie.

"Of course, dear." Mrs. Hattie smiled knowingly. "And how is his shop? Still running like a machine, I suppose? He always kept it in tiptop shape."

"His shop is fine. Very well maintained," she said.

"Oh, I bet. That man is a marvel," she said, her words laced with an affection that told her she most definitely was not talking about Jackson's garage.

"Mrs. Hattie!" Allison stared at her in shock.

"I'd climb him like a tree, dear. Damn these bad hips," Mrs. Hattie mused, grasping her hips, a wistful smile on her lips. The woman walked away humming to herself. All Allison could do was stare after her, pretending that her own thoughts had not strayed to the same place.

"I really just want to find a place and open a nail shop," Jamila said with a wistful smile. "But it's not a straightforward task to do in a small town where no one really knows or trusts you."

"Have you found anything for rent yet?" Allison asked.

Jamila shook her head. "I've seen a couple of places, but no one has taken me seriously yet. I feel like my skin color is working against me," she said with a scoff. "Linda's been great. She even gave me a raise so I can put down a bigger down payment, but I have no clue about negotiating."

"I can look at the contracts if you want. It's part of my actual job, and it would be a nice change of pace," Allison offered.

Jamila waved her off. "I don't want to take advantage of a friend. Besides, I'd need someone to offer me a contract first. Don't worry about it. I'll figure it out."

She moved to the next rack of clothing and started browsing dresses. Allison still wanted to help despite her friend's refusal. Maybe she could do some research on her own tonight. In a small town, it shouldn't be too hard to find the open real estate spots and who owned them. Maybe Jackson even knew a few of the owners.

Her mind wandered to Jackson and suddenly she transported back to last night on his porch steps, remembering the feel of his hands on her skin, the roughness of his fingertips against her flesh.

"Alright, what's up?" Jamila said from the other side of the clothing rack, and Allison looked up. The two had gone shopping that morning as a distraction from Allison's ongoing "daydream" issues, and here she was already daydreaming.

Allison tried to play dumb with a shrug. "What do you mean?"

"Girl, you've been staring at that same shirt for ten minutes, and it's not even your size." She glanced at the yellow tank top with pink ruffles. Allison closed her eyes and let out an exasperated sigh before hanging it back on the rack.

Jamila continued to gaze at her with a raised brow. Biting her lip, Allison took a deep breath before confessing. "I kissed Jackson."

She corrected herself. "Well, he kissed me first, and then I kissed him the next day."

"Wait, two days of kissing?" her friend asked for clarification.

Allison felt overwhelmed and walked to the edge of the store and sat down on a chair, shaking her head as Jamila approached. "I fell at the creek, and I guess it scared him and the next thing I knew, he was kissing me. I was too shocked to react at first, but then I kissed him back," she growled. "No matter how irritated that makes me feel."

Jamila chuckled. "Honey, I think that's just part of your foreplay."

She blew out an angry breath. "Then last night, I went to his place to deliver that food Linda asked me to, and—" Allison was mumbling. Jamila leaned in to hear her better. "Okay, fine, as I was leaving, I kissed him, and damn, it was hot as hell."

Jamila squealed and bounced on her toes. "So, just a good-night kiss. Or was there more?"

Allison could feel herself starting to blush. "It was more than just a kiss, but I stopped it from going any further. He was definitely—" she leaned closer to her friend and whispered, "aroused."

"Girl, you left him hanging?" she exclaimed, and Allison quickly placed her hand over her friend's mouth to silence her.

"I think he can handle himself, Jamila. He's not a teenager," she said. "I wasn't going to sleep with him."

"Why the heck not?" she asked. Allison glanced around to make sure they weren't causing a scene. The last thing she needed was to become the next big gossip story of Titusville. "He's attractive. Why wouldn't you want that? Clearly, he's into you."

"Because I'm not looking for a one-night stand. I wasn't even supposed to stay this long," she said. Reaching up, she rubbed the back of her neck, which was getting tense.

Jamila shook her head and made a disapproving sound. "You're better than me, girl," she said. "That man has never even looked my direction, but if he did, I would have tapped it so hard."

Allison couldn't deny her temptation. After all, it wasn't like she hadn't hooked up with men before; that was how she had met Chip, after all. Men were allowed to blow off steam, so why was it something that women were looked down on for doing? "I don't know," Allison said. "He's still so annoying."

"Girl, I didn't tell you to have a conversation with him," Jamila said. "There are plenty of things Jackson Lancaster could do to you that have little to do with talking."

With a wink, Jamila walked back to the clothing rack, leaving Allison alone to consider exactly what those things were.

Lying in bed that evening, Allison wondered why she had avoided going to the shop that day. Was she truly unable to control herself around Jackson?

And why hadn't she gone back to Erie yet? She was dragging her feet now. Tomorrow would be one week since she had come to town, and all she had done was teach him a few phrases and how to enter line items in his program on his computer.

Growling, she covered her head with her comforter and closed her eyes. Tomorrow, she needed to go to the shop and finish the job. Stop screwing around and just make sure he had everything he needed so she could go home to Erie.

Her phone buzzed on her nightstand, and she peeked out to glance at it, only to groan in frustration at finding Chip's name on the screen. Oh yeah, she needed to explain to her boss why Jackson wasn't going to sell the shop to her.

Picking up the phone, she glanced at the text.

Chip

> Checking in on your progress

Chip

> Been researching our mutual subject, Jackson

Chip

> His injuries are pretty extensive. I got his hospital records. dont ask questions.

Chip

> Sending them to your email

Chip

its a good angle to go after.

Chip

Also found this article on the brother Dylan

Chip

Alot of trouble from that kid last year, sending it to your email

Chip

Walking disaster. no way he stays sober long enough to help him keep that place afloat. push there.

Allison

Thanks I'll look at it tonight

Chip

Make sure you do

Chip

Counting on you Allie Cat

Allison sighed as she reached for her laptop, opening her email to find the files that Chip had sent to her. She didn't know who he had sweet-talked at the hospital to get Jackson's medical records, but it was highly illegal. HIPAA anyone?

Clicking into the file, she winced at the pictures of his face—they must have been taken immediately after the accident.

Blood covered Jackson's face; gashes across his cheek and chin cut to the bone. She thought the scar under his chin must have come from that night. On the next page was a photo of the motorcycle scattered across a road, pieces of it still stuck in a tree. It was a wonder he had survived something like that.

Skimming through the records, she read about talks of surgery and a broken femur. He had rods placed in his leg to fix the break. Jackson had been in the hospital for four weeks, where he went through rigorous physical therapy treatments and learned to walk again.

He suffered second-degree burns to his chest and hip, along with a few broken ribs. Feeling suddenly nauseous from reading, she clicked out of the file and into the article Chip sent.

The article was about a fight that had taken place at Boondocks Bar last year between Dylan Lancaster, Blake Forrester, and Casey Anderson, the pitcher for the Pittsburgh Pirates. For a small town, this place sure had some excitement last year. The article only stated that a fight had broken out between the three men, and that all three had been arrested and taken to the sheriff's department for questioning. The article suggested alcohol played a role that evening, and that all charges had been dismissed.

Closing her laptop, she wasn't sure what Chip wanted her to do with that information. Clearly, Dylan and his friend Blake had taken issue with Casey, but she didn't know how that related to Jackson or the shop.

She hated using any of this information against the Lancasters. None of it changed the fact that Jackson wasn't going to sell his shop. Perhaps if she just went in there tomorrow and finished what she come to do, she could leave and tell Chip she did everything she could but failed. Sure, she'd have to work under Larry for a while, but Chip would get over his hissy fit, eventually.

Would Chip actually ruin her career over this?

Allison felt torn. How had she gotten stuck in this situation? And why did she care so much about what happened to Jackson Lancaster and his auto shop?

Chapter Fifteen

Jackson

J ax was sitting at his desk Thursday morning, tapping at the keyboard as he entered the invoices into his computer, when his brother, Dylan, walked into the room, staring at him with a scowl on his face. "And how can I help you?" Jax asked, pulling the glasses down onto the tip of his nose.

His brother responded, "How about you start by explaining what you're doing?"

"Well, I'm entering all our expenses for the week, and I learned this really neat trick." He pressed the enter key and watched as the item popped up on the screen. "See, there it is. Just like it's supposed to do. No beeping," he responded with a giant grin.

Dylan stared at him, clearly unimpressed. "I mean with Allison."

Jax chuckled. "What about Allison?"

"What's going on with you two?" Dylan asked. "Because I don't trust her!"

Jax scooted back from his desk, staring at his brother in confusion. "What are you talking about?"

"Why is she even here? She should have gone home already, and yet she's still sniffing around. What's the point? If you don't want to learn anything else, send her packing." Dylan paused briefly. "Unless there's another reason you don't want her gone."

"Of course I want her gone, Dyl. She's a pain in the ass."

"Really? Then what's with the shirt?" Dylan stared at him suspiciously.

Jax glanced at his shirt, then back up at his brother. "What's wrong with my shirt?"

Dylan raised an eyebrow. "Really, Jax? Since when have you worn a button-down to the garage?" He leaned over and sniffed the air, adding with an air of disgust, "Is that cologne?"

Jax scoffed and shrugged. "Is there a problem with wanting to look or smell good?"

"Look good for who? You work in a garage with your brother where you sweat all day!" His voice raised freely as he flung his arms around. The garage door opened and closed, and Dylan turned toward the noise. Allison walked toward the office, and Jax glanced up at his brother the moment she entered the room with a warning glance.

"Morning, boys," she greeted cheerily.

Dylan grunted in response, and Jax shot him a dirty look. "Morning, Allison. I wondered if maybe you left town after you didn't stop by yesterday." The thought had crossed his mind, weighing on him more than expected.

"Didn't think you'd get rid of me that easily, did you, Jackson?" She smiled, though he recognized she seemed nervous.

"Where would the fun in that be?" he teased, maintaining eye contact with her.

She chuckled and started to respond before his brother groaned loudly. "Oh, for fuck's sake," Dylan cursed, causing them both to turn in his direction. "I can't do this today. I'm gonna go pick up food." He stormed out of the office, slamming the garage door on the way out.

"What was that about?" Allison asked once they were alone.

"Got his panties in a twist this morning, I don't know." Jax shrugged, pushing his glasses back up onto his nose. "So, what am I learning today?"

She blinked in surprise. "Oh, um, your enthusiasm is not exactly what I expected."

Jax humorously held out his arms and flashed a cheeky smile. "I am but your humble student. Teach me."

Narrowing her eyes, she stared at him suspiciously. "Who are you, and what have you done with Jackson Lancaster?" She looked around the room with a smile. "Is he tied up in your cabin? Blink twice if you are under duress."

"I assure you, it's still cranky ole me," he said, standing up to grab another chair for her. However, he paused when his knee turned in the wrong direction, momentarily causing it to buckle under him. Closing his eyes, he frowned, holding up his finger to pause her as she advanced toward him. "I'm fine." After feeling like he had his bearings under him, he stepped toward the corner of the room, grabbed the chair, and brought it over to the desk before setting it down. "Have a seat."

Tentatively, she sat down and observed him. "Are you sure..."

He laughed. "I'm not gonna break. Hell, part of me is made of metal." He tapped his fist on the side of his leg where the metal rods were placed. "You might as well call me Iron Man."

"Have you ever thought about doing something else besides this?" she asked tentatively. "I'm sure it would be easier to get around, less stress on your leg not to have to work in a garage all day."

He shook his head firmly. "Nah, this was my dream ever since I started working here with my dad as a boy."

"But there have to be other dreams, things that—"

He was quick to cut her off. "No Allison, what part aren't you getting? This is it for me. Either I make this work, or I fail, but this is my life."

Digging into the top drawer of his desk, he pulled out a photo of him and his dad. He couldn't remember how old he was, maybe four or five, but he was sitting on the shop counter in overalls, holding a plastic wrench and a screwdriver while his dad stood beside him. Looking at the picture, he explained, "I fought to keep this place because of him. Because of what he taught me. And hell, I know I may not be the smartest guy in the world, but I'm no quitter. And I'll be damned if I'm gonna let one stupid accident ruin my life. One day, my dad is going to walk back into this place and tell me I made him proud."

She stared at him, and he sensed something deeper behind her eyes that she was holding back. After a moment, she blinked and nodded. "Alright then, let's make sure you don't fail."

"Thank you," he said honestly, turning back to his computer. "I actually had a question, and I'm not sure if you are the right person to ask."

She stared at him in surprise, and then stumbled with a response. "Y ... you have a question for me?"

"Stop looking at me like that. I have actual business questions," he said, shaking his head before turning back to his computer. "We get all our parts out of Pittsburgh, but I've been looking at our current parts cost percentage compared to the total revenue. I'm trying to figure out if that's something I should negotiate with a different supplier or not. My dad always used the same company for the last fifteen years, but maybe it's time I look at making better deals."

He handed her the printout, and she scanned it over with her eyes. "Auto parts aren't exactly my expertise, but it's never a bad idea to negotiate better market prices with suppliers. You could have one that provides you a discount for years of service, or taking advantage of you because of the changeover from business partners now that your dad has left." She pointed to a few of the line items. "See how these have increased in the last six months? That's about the time you took over. You could call that out, see what they say about it, maybe they give you a break on the price if you tell them you're looking elsewhere," she suggested with a laugh. "It's always about having leverage or knowing the weakness of the guy on the other end of the phone."

"Damn, didn't realize your business was like the mafia. You want a job? I probably can't pay you half of what you make at your job, but I could always make it up in the benefits package," he joked, winking playfully.

She rolled her eyes and pushed the printouts back into his hand. "I'm not looking for a new job, Jackson."

"You didn't ask me what kind of benefits we were talking about." He winked and watched a pink blush form on her cheeks.

"You're ridiculous." She laughed as she stood up and reached for a printout of something she had researched on the computer. He took a moment to watch her as she read over the document. Her hair was loosely braided and tied at the back of her neck, with a few tendrils framing her face and draping across her forehead. As she twirled a piece of hair between her fingers, she read the paper. The rest of her copper locks hung freely under the braid, loosely lying against the back of her flowered tank top. He had a sudden desire to run his fingers through her hair.

She looked up, and he quickly stared back at the computer, clearing his voice. "Uh, so besides negotiating with suppliers, anything else I should do differently?"

"You might want to take a look at turnaround times." She handed him the page in her hand. "Nothing against your brother, but he seems to flake out a lot." He grunted his dissatisfaction with her statement, but he had to acknowledge that she wasn't wrong. "I know you're the only shop in town, so people have to be willing to wait for however long you take, but it could affect your revenue potential if another shop ever opened up or competition in another town suddenly became an issue."

"Dylan's *my* problem," he said firmly, doing a double take as she leaned over him, giving him a clear view of her bra beneath her shirt.

"Of course!" she said. "Just pointing out potential problems and areas you might want to focus on."

"Well, I appreciate all the advice, truly," he said, standing up and crossing the room. "I know I haven't exactly shown that the whole time." Reaching on top of the file cabinet, he flipped on the radio, as the chorus of Alice Cooper's "Poison" filtered through the speakers.

She smiled. "Really, I hadn't noticed." She reached up and pulled her hair away from her neck, her fingers dipping into her amber locks.

"Yeah, well, sometimes I can be difficult," he said with a smirk. He pushed a tendril of her hair behind her ear. He observed her swallow and blink slowly. "My mother used to say that was part of my charm."

She replied softly, licking her lips, "That's because mothers always think their children do no wrong."

"My mother thought I was a stubborn son of a bitch actually." He grinned, trailing his thumb along her neck as her eyes closed. "But there was one thing she taught me," he said, his voice dropping to nearly a whisper.

When she opened her eyes, her voice was so soft he could barely hear her as she spoke. "What's that?"

"Never let someone leave without showing your appreciation for them when they do something nice for you." Leaning in, he tenderly brushed his lips against her neck, his breath warm against her skin as she let out a soft moan. "And I always listened to my mama," he whispered.

She squeezed his bicep with her right hand; her nails digging into his shirtsleeves as he dragged his teeth along her jaw. "Jackson, I'm not sure..." she whimpered as their lips met. He backed her against the desk, gripping her hips as he lifted her onto the desktop.

Her delicate fingers tangled in his hair, pulling him closer as he settled between her legs. He licked the inside of her mouth, savoring the sensation of her tongue against his. A growl escaped his throat as he ran his hand up her side, slipping it under her tank top. She arched into his touch, inviting him to explore further as his hand inched along her chest, tracing the lace at the edge of her bra.

His fingers danced delicately between the flesh of her skin and the soft lacey material, playfully teasing the line he was hesitant to cross. She moaned his name softly and her hand guided his over her bra, pressing it against her breast. Locking eyes with her, he sensed no hesitation as he leaned in, pressing his lips to hers in a heated kiss.

With a gentle touch, he explored beneath the lacy fabric to find her hardened nipple, causing her to moan with a desire he had been thinking about for hours. She wrapped her legs around him, tugging him closer. The heat of their bodies causing his arousal to grow.

Allison pulled back and removed her top, revealing a black lace bra, as Jax gazed at her with intensity. With a sly grin, he leaned down and brushed his lips just above her bra, savoring the velvety texture of her skin. Skillfully, he unclasped the bra with a flick of his fingers *(he was still good at that, he noted)*, freeing the straps to slide down her arms.

He was a man on a mission as he lowered his head and gently kissed her breast, his tongue teasing her firm nipple. Allison's grip tightened in his hair, her nails lightly scratching his scalp. He looked up at her and was captivated by her gaze, her intense eyes fixed on his. He smirked while drawing her nipple into his mouth, observing her eyes close and her head tilt back, softly whimpering his name.

Damn, he could watch that on repeat all day long.

Those lips of hers, so perfectly plump and wet, he wanted them everywhere. He was straining against his pants just thinking about those pretty lips touching him intimately. When she opened her eyes again, he wrapped a hand around the back of her neck and pressed his mouth to those lips, growling in an explosion of yearning he hadn't felt in years.

Suddenly, she pulled away. "Jackson, I should tell you something." Biting her lip, she stared up at him.

"Let me guess, you have a husband and three kids back home," he teased.

She slapped playfully at his chest. "No, it's about my boss..."

"I don't enjoy talking about other men when I'm kissing a woman." He silenced her with another kiss, one hand sliding into her hair as the other pressed firmly against her breast.

Her fingers were desperately tugging at the buttons of his shirt when a sudden crash outside the office disrupted the moment. Frozen in place, they listened intently over the sound of their ragged breaths. With her face buried in his neck, he heard another crash and then suddenly, Dylan cursed.

He swore under his breath, frustrated by the interruption. Handing her shirt to her, he decided he needed to check on the situation before Dylan barged into the office. "I'll go see what's going on." He adjusted himself, ran a hand through his hair, and stepped out, closing the door behind him. Dylan was going to owe him big time for this!

"Dyl, what the fuck are you doing out here?" he yelled into the empty garage, searching for his brother but finding nothing but empty darkness. "Dylan?"

On the other side of the room, his brother stood up and stumbled toward him. "Still working, bro?" Dylan laughed with a light hiccup. "Of course you are, gotta be Dad's hero, right?"

"Are you drunk?" he asked, sighing.

"What do you think?" He tripped and fell over a random part lying on the floor and Jax rushed forward to pick him up.

There was blood on his forehead and a gash in his hand from where he had braced himself from falling. "Ah hell, bro, what the hell are you doing?" Jax asked in aggravation.

"Get your hands off me," he growled, shoving Jackson. The moment he stepped back, his leg hit the concrete at a weird angle, causing it to give out as he tumbled against the counter and fell to the ground with a loud crash.

Chapter Sixteen

Allison

A llison pulled her tank top over her head after securing her bra, then bent over to look at her hair in the dirty mirror in the corner to fix it. What in the hell was she thinking, acting like a horny teenager with no self-control? Was she truly considering having sex with Jackson Lancaster on top of his desk in a dirty auto shop garage?

Her emotions had been out of control all day, especially after receiving the threat from Chip. Looking down at her phone, she re-read the message.

Chip

I haven't heard from you again

Chip

I'm getting tired of your incompetence Allie

Chip

If you don't get this done, Larry will be the least of your concerns

Chip

Either you take care of this, or I'll do it for you

Chip

I expect a response!!

Closing her eyes, she groaned. She finished dressing just as she heard another loud crash from the other side of the door. Hurrying out, she reached the scene in time to witness Dylan standing over his brother and Jackson lying on the ground. Rushing to Jackson's side, she kneeled down to check on him. "What happened?" she asked.

"My idiot brother happened," Jackson growled.

"Of course *you're* still here," Dylan, glaring at Allison, snapped. "Why don't you just go back home where you belong?"

Jackson, now sitting up, rubbed the back of his head. Allison gently examined him to ensure he was alright. "Leave her out of this, Dylan," Jackson said, pushing himself up onto his feet.

Dylan continued angrily. "Why is she involved? Why does she even care about this shop, Jax?" The tension rose, and Allison felt uncomfortable under Dylan's intense gaze.

"I wish you cared about this shop a bit more. You're always running off to get drunk," Jackson said, glaring at his brother as Dylan refused to cower and instead only seemed to grow bolder in his anger.

"Why do you care where I am? No one gives a shit where I am. Everyone leaves Jax, everyone. Dad, Sam, Blake ... Mom! No one cares about us, they all leave! And now you ... with her!" Allison felt like an outsider witnessing a deeply personal moment until he turned and glared at her. Dylan was crying now, but she could tell he did not know he was even doing so. The anger was visceral, and the way he was swaying on his feet told her he had more than enough alcohol that evening to knock him off his feet.

Dylan collapsed on himself, falling backward against a red pickup truck that was sitting in the bay waiting for parts. Jackson rushed forward to wrap his arms around his brother, cradling him against his body as they both slid to the ground. Dylan lay there against his chest, and Jackson looked up at her, his eyes helplessly seeking hers for some sort of guidance. "I'm sorry, Dylan. I'm sorry, bro," Jackson murmured against the top of his brother's head.

"I'll get him a bottle of water," she said, stepping back toward the office. She had read the article about Dylan, showing he may have had anger issues or been out with a friend who had too much to drink. But this situation was different. Dylan was obviously going through something serious, and there was no way Allison could exploit that or use it against them. Dylan needed his brother, his family, and serious help.

Returning to the brothers, she handed Jackson the bottle of water. "Thanks," he said as she stepped back. "You think you can help me get him up?" She placed her hand under Dylan's arm and helped lift him from the ground as Jackson did the same.

"Is he gonna be alright?" she asked.

"Yeah," he said. "I hate to ask, but do you think you could help me get him home?"

She smiled softly. "Of course."

"Thanks, he's dead weight when he's drunk, and my knee can't support him up his stairs," Jackson explained with a sad look on his face.

"Jackson, it's fine. Anyone drunk is hard to deal with by yourself," she said, hoping he wouldn't feel inadequate in the situation.

Jackson then leaned his brother against the truck. "I'll go get the keys. Be right back."

Standing alone with Dylan, she noticed him staring at the floor, his eyes fixated on his shoes. "Your brother cares a lot about you," she said.

Dylan shot back angrily, "Why does any of this matter to you?"

"I don't have any siblings. I always wanted a brother or a sister. I've never had anyone whose had my back. In fact, I don't even know what that feels like. You're pretty lucky to have someone who is there no matter what, even when you make bad choices. That's pretty rare."

"Is that why you're here, then? Trying to steal my family? Or just our shop?" he said, raising the accusation like a sword.

With guilt sitting on the back of her mind, she exhaled. "I'm not here to steal your shop, Dylan. I just wanted to help your father and Jackson."

He simply shook his head and growled. "Whatever, I still don't trust you."

"Yeah, me either," she muttered as Jackson returned to her side, wrapping his arm around his brother's back to help bring Dylan to the car.

Allison observed as Jackson carefully tucked Dylan into bed, ensuring that his brother had everything he might need if he woke up during the night. He placed a bottle of aspirin on the bedside table, a glass of water, and even a bucket within reach before stepping away and switching off the lights.

Dylan lived in an apartment above the main house's garage, a space that seemed small and well-lived-in, yet not quite suitable for someone his age. The room contained a bed in one corner, a tiny kitchenette, and a chair facing a television. She struggled to imagine Dylan being content in such a confined space.

She noticed the pile of notebooks sitting on the table and flipped one open to reveal some pencil drawings of old cars. They were quite impressive. She flipped through a few pages, each one a look inside Dylan's brain as the drawings grew more and more intricate and dark.

"I think he's asleep now," Jackson said, startling her and causing her to slam the book shut.

Allison nodded and followed Jackson down the small stairs toward the back of the house where Dylan's private entrance was located. "Is he going to be alright?" she asked as they exited the apartment and Jackson closed the door behind them.

"Yeah, he'll sleep it off and feel like an asshole in the morning," Jackson said with a chuckle, causing her to frown.

"Does he do this often?" she asked.

Jackson started walking the small path back to the front of the house. "You know, back when Blake lived here, they would go out on the weekends, have a few drinks, take the piss out on some asshole for being stupid, but they never got drunk like this. It was just friends being morons. This is different," Jackson said.

She hesitated to bring up the arrest. She was worried it might appear as if she had researched Dylan. "When did it start?" she finally asked.

He ran his hand through his hair, a gesture she recognized as a sign of his frustration. "Probably when Blake moved away. Losing Blake and Dad has been tough on him. I thought he'd be okay here with me. But I don't think he envisioned this life for himself. Living above the garage, fixing cars, sleeping with chicks he ain't got no business being around," he sighed. "He's slowly destroying himself with his own unhappiness."

There were so many other things she wanted to ask, but she didn't know how to ask without feeling like she was manipulating the situation. If Dylan didn't want to work at the shop, though, how was Jackson supposed to run any of it? She was trying to convince herself that she wanted to ask him questions out of genuine concern for Jackson's wellbeing, but a part of her wasn't sure if her own ulterior motives weren't somehow mixed in there. She turned toward him. "Jackson—"

He suddenly interrupted. "You hungry?"

"What?"

He grinned. "Let me take you to dinner." He reached out to brush his fingers along her arm, leaving goosebumps in their wake. Watching his hand trail over her skin, she felt the fire of his touch and swallowed the desire she felt for him. Sleeping with Jackson was a bad idea.

"I don't know," she said reluctantly. "I don't think it's a good idea."

He teased childishly, "Eating isn't a good idea? Is it dangerous? Are you afraid I'll poison you?"

"No, that's not what I meant, and you know it."

"Come on, Allison, it's just dinner. I'll take you to Linda's if that makes you feel safer." His innocent grin and windswept hair made her stomach do somersaults, but she knew this was a mistake. Biting her lip, she rocked slightly on her feet. "Listen, I'll even let you pay." He grinned widely.

She snorted. "Wow, how very forward thinking of you!"

He chuckled. "I just want you to feel comfortable. After all, you make more money in this relationship."

She pointed between them. "This is not a relationship."

"Exactly, it's just dinner, which you are buying." Extending his arm, he stared down at her. "What do you say, Firefly?"

She sighed heavily. "Fine, but I'm not sleeping with you."

He let out a very loud noise and opened his eyes wide. "Allison Hanover, are you propositioning me? I'll have you know I never sleep with a woman on the first date." He shook his head in mock disgust. "Women these days are so forward."

Playfully, she slapped his arm and followed him toward his truck. This man was going to be the end of her.

Sitting at Linda's Diner with Jackson Lancaster in the booth across from her felt improper, but also strangely exhilaratingly. She stared down at the menu but kept looking up as his knee bumped against hers under the table. "What are you doing?" she asked after the fourth time.

"What?" he asked innocently.

"You know what you're doing." She stared at him without blinking.

He grinned and glanced under the table. "Was that your leg? Sorry, I thought it was the table."

"Jackson, behave," she scolded.

"What a wonderful surprise." Jamila's voice interrupted them as she walked up to the table. "What brings you two in here ... *together*?"

"Food! We're just here for food," Allison said clearly.

"I'm *starving*, that's for sure," Jackson answered, his voice dark and his eyes never leaving hers, making her entire body light on fire.

Jamila glanced between them. "Do you need another minute with the menu or?"

"I'll just take my salad," she said with a polite smile.

Jackson didn't even look at the menu as he continued to stare at her. "Burger and fries, no onions please. Thanks, J."

Jamila glanced at Allison and winked. "Be right up, you two."

As soon as they were alone again, Allison grinned and tried to distract Jackson with light conversation. "So, how long were Dylan and Blake friends?"

"They were toddlers. I swear those two were inseparable as kids." He laughed. "Sam, Blake, and Dylan were only a couple of years apart in age, so the three of them were always together growing up. We went camping together as families and spent every holiday together. Honestly, I don't remember not being around the Forresters growing up."

"Did Sam and Blake date when they were growing up?" she asked.

"Hell no, I don't think anyone knew Sam even liked Blake until last year, especially not Blake," he said with a nod.

"That must have been shocking for Dylan." The pieces of why Dylan might be struggling the past few months were making more sense.

Jackson snorted. "Let's just say he took it as well as you might expect for a loveable asshole with control issues when it comes to his sister and his best friend." Shaking his head, he continued, "He's fine with it now, I think. I mean, they talk on the phone, he texts his sister every damn morning. But it was a lot of people to lose all at once when they moved to New York."

"Do you think it might be a good idea for Dylan to go visit her?" she asked.

"I've been thinking about that honestly. It's not a bad idea, but I feel like I'm just pushing him off on her instead of dealing with the issue myself," he said.

"I don't think anyone expects you to be a hero." She shrugged. "But if he's not happy here, I can't see him getting any better sticking around." She bit her lip. She knew this next question should come organically, but it felt wrong of her to ask it, considering all the other ulterior motives she had. "What would you do about the shop if Dylan wasn't here to help you?"

"Yeah, I'd have to figure that out, but my brother's health is more important than anything else, right?"

Jamila interrupted them with their order, setting the food between them, ending the conversation. Jackson was right, of course. Dylan's health was more important than anything else. And that included Chip wanting to get his hands on Jackson Lancaster's shop.

Chapter Seventeen

Jackson

J ax opened the passenger side door of his truck and Allison hopped inside. He slammed the door shut behind her and walked around to the other side before climbing in. It had been an interesting evening to put it lightly.

Throughout the dinner conversation, he had either felt completely emotionally unstable about the discussion they were having about his brother or had spent it thinking about having sex with the woman on the other side of the table. Allison Hanover had a way of bringing out the most conflicting emotions in him.

As he turned the key in the ignition and tapped on the steering wheel, he flipped on the radio and closed his eyes the moment the soft sounds of "Iris" by the Goo Goo Dolls started playing through his speakers.

Sometimes music was a goddamn bitch.

"So, uh, should I take you back to your car now?" he asked.

She glanced at him and then back at the road. "Actually, I was thinking maybe we could go have a beer ... back at your place."

Surprised by her suggestion, and once again with his thoughts returning to sex, he tightened his grip on the steering wheel. "Miss Hanover, are you asking me to take you back to my cabin on the first date? Because that seems awfully—"

She interrupted him with a mischievous grin. "Are you trying to change my mind?"

He wasn't about to argue with a woman flirting with him. "You don't have to tell me twice, Firefly." He pressed his foot on the accelerator, turning down the road toward his cabin.

Of course, the drive back to his cabin seemed endless, with each mile feeling like ten. He wasn't sure what tonight would bring. Allison wasn't exactly an open book. A beer back at his place could literally mean what she said, a beer and conversation that turned into an argument or ... well, Jax was almost embarrassed at how giddy with anticipation he was thinking about what exactly "or" could mean.

Once he pulled into the driveway, he paused before turning off the engine. They sat in silence, gazing at the cabin. After a moment, he mustered the courage to ask, "You still want that beer?"

She nodded silently, reaching for the door handle, and sliding out of the truck. He followed suit, closing the door with a slam as he made his way toward the cabin. As he approached the door, his mind raced with his own anxious thoughts.

Had he done the dishes?

Was his laundry put away or did he leave it in the basket on the couch?

While he was a thirty-something-year-old bachelor, he didn't exactly want to look like a slob.

He pushed the door open, greeted by the dog excitedly jumping around at his feet. "Hey, boy, did you miss me?" After letting the dog out, he was relieved to see the living room was tidy. At least he had remembered to be an adult this week. "I'll grab the beer if you want to have a seat," he suggested, gesturing toward the couch.

"Alright," she replied, taking a seat while he excused himself to the kitchen.

Leaning forward on the counter, he closed his eyes and exhaled. He didn't want to mess things up with Allison. It wasn't every day a guy like him could land a chick like Allison Hanover. She was way out of his league, pretty, smart, sophisticated, yet here she was sitting in his living room. He was determined not to let a once-in-a-lifetime opportunity like this slip away.

He grabbed two beers and paused at the front door to let his dog back in. Allison sat up, reaching for her beer as Jax joined her on the couch. She took a sip, hiding her sour expression this time. He chuckled. "You're getting better at that."

"At what?" she asked.

"Pretending you enjoy drinking beer," he replied with a smile, gesturing to the bottle in her hand.

"It's an acquired taste," she teased, obviously remembering their last discussion on the porch. He tilted the bottle back and drank his beer as she observed him. "Did you get that in your accident?" she asked, tentatively reaching out to brush her fingers against his chin, lightly grazing his jaw along the spot where his stitches had healed months prior.

He nodded silently, a soft murmur of admission leaving his lips as her fingers continued to trace his jaw, brushing against the stubble on his chin. "Ten stitches," he responded hoarsely.

"And this?" She ran a finger along his cheek to the light scar there. He nodded again. Their eyes locked on each other. His fingers undid the top four buttons of his shirt, watching her as each one slid through the hole.

He reached up and clasped her hand in his, dragging it to his chest and placing her palm against his flesh as he dragged it further down his side. "Thirty-six stitches, right here." Her fingers danced along the trail of his scar, reverently tracing the puckered line of flesh along his abs. Pulling her hand across his chest, he slid it to the other side, stopping at the long gash below his ribs. "Three broken ribs."

"Was it painful?" she asked, her eyes gazing over his chest.

"Hurt like a son of a bitch." He chuckled. She traced the line against his chest, her fingers dancing along the scar, igniting every nerve in his body. With a gentle and loving touch, she brushed his hair away from his face as her hand caressed his cheek. Their eyes met, and before he could react, she began unbuttoning the rest of the buttons of his shirt. Sliding her hands along his shoulders, she eased the material off his back and down his arms.

Her gaze lingered on his chest, taking in every detail, every scrape and scar. He felt completely exposed. He closed his eyes as she kissed his shoulder softly, causing a soft moan to escape his throat.

As her mouth moved to his chest, he lifted her face, their lips meeting in a kiss that ignited a fire between them.

His hands swiftly moved through her hair and then to her shirt, pulling it off and throwing it to the floor, revealing that tantalizing and maddening black lace bra. "This thing could be lethal to a man, you know," he groaned, teasing the lace with his fingers.

"Oh, really?" She stared at him, unclasping her bra and letting it fall to the ground. "Then perhaps I should get rid of it."

Jax took a deep breath as he took in her bare breasts. "That is so much better," he said with a smirk. He stood up, taking her hands in his, leading her backward through the living room toward his bedroom.

Standing on her tiptoes, she placed her hands on his shoulders, her bare chest against his as she kissed his neck. He hit the doorframe with his shoulder, grunting momentarily until her tongue slid into his ear, distracting him from the inconsequential pain. As she lifted her leg, he grasped her thigh, pressing her against him as he groaned and nipped at her earlobe. "I have other scars you can explore," he said. "If that's what gets you off."

"Really?" she moaned, teasing the waistband of his pants. "Maybe you should show me?"

Grasping her hand, he drew it along the front of his pants, pressing against the hard ridges of his erection. She sucked in a deep breath. "Settle down, Allison, he's perfectly intact." He dragged her hand further down his thigh. "But the rest of my leg, not so much."

"I don't care about any of that," she whispered, tracing the outline of his bulge with her fingers. He leaned back against the doorframe, closing his eyes with a groan. "This, however, has my attention."

"Yeah? I think he's very interested in you," he whispered as he kissed her neck, his hands moving to her waist. He pushed off the wall and guided her into the dimly lit bedroom. As she approached him, her breasts subtly swayed in the moonlight. His heart started speeding faster than a racecar driver approaching the finish line. "I uh, I'm just gonna..." He gestured toward the restroom. "Make yourself comfortable."

He walked to the bathroom, closed the door behind him, and allowed himself a moment of panic. Opening his cabinet drawers, he searched through them. Condoms. Surely, he had condoms. This wasn't something he did often, especially since his accident. In fact, he hadn't been naked in front of any woman since the doctors had butchered and stitched him back up.

Running his hand through his hair, he nervously shut one drawer and opened the last one at the bottom, relieved to find the box of condoms nestled at the back of the drawer. Thank God for small miracles. Placing a silver packet on the counter, he undressed down to his boxers, picked up the packet, and left the bathroom, trying to bury his nervous energy.

He swallowed thickly when he entered the bedroom, seeing Allison stretched out on his bed in just a pair of black lace panties, her amber hair spread out across his checkered sheets.

She was damn near the hottest thing that had ever been in his bed.

He held up the condom and raised his brow, walking over and setting it on the nightstand. She stared at him, her eyes glancing up and down his body, and suddenly he felt very exposed.

His eyes traced her long, toned legs. He pulled her foot up his body, massaging her calf with his hand before bending to press his lips where his hands had been. With his knee on the mattress, his fingers continued their way toward the apex of her thigh, his mouth not far behind as he peppered ardent kisses to each part of her flesh. He reached for her panties, gently tugging them down her body, until he revealed her most intimate places inch by inch.

As she lay bare in front of him, the sight of the stunning woman in his bed humbled him, and he felt an overwhelming desire to worship every inch of her skin. "Never seen a naked woman before?" she teased, gazing up at him.

Leaning over to plant a gentle kiss on her stomach, he gazed into her eyes. "I've encountered my fair share of naked women. Hell, I ain't no saint, Allison." His lips blazed a fiery trail along her abdomen. "But my eyes have never seen anything quite like you before."

"Oh, really?" she challenged him, playfully biting her finger. "Is that a criticism or a compliment?"

"To be honest, I'm not even sure how I ended up with you in this bed." Bringing his lips to hers, she took a deep breath. "I don't know if this is pity or something else, and I might be broken," he murmured, his tongue gliding along her neck as he drew closer. "But I have no intention of holding back tonight."

Her hands ran through his hair, her nails lightly scratching his scalp. "You've never been gentle with me before today, Jackson, and I don't expect you to start now." She grinned. "But if you believe this is out of pity," she playfully nibbled on his earlobe, "then you have underestimated me, because I don't give my pity to anyone."

Placing her hands on either side of his face, she brought their mouths together. Her tongue slipped past his lips into his mouth, the intensity of her desire evident in the fervor of their kiss.

Jax felt his arousal building against the growing heat between her legs. It would be so easy to remove his boxers and sink into her, but he wanted more. He needed to savor this. For all he knew, this was the last night he would have Allison before she went back to Erie.

He slid slowly down her body, his tongue marking a fiery trail along her salty skin, lingering only to savor the firmness of her pert nipples and the soft curves of her breasts, which responded eagerly to his touch.

He yearned to explore every inch of her, to savor her throughout the night. His hand pressed against her thigh, sliding between her legs until he reached the spot he had been dying to touch. The moment he did, he found her wet and writhing beneath him. Her eyes met his as his finger slid inside of her, and a moan left her mouth so sensual and deep that he thought he might ruin everything and explode in his boxers right then and there. "Oh God, Jackson." She groaned, pinching her eyes shut.

His name on her lips sounded so sweet. He needed to hear it again.

She gripped his shoulder, her nails digging into his skin as he pumped his fingers inside of her, watching her with intense curiosity, as if he was mentally taking notes on which movements elicited each sound, just waiting for the one that had her panting his name.

Smirking against her breast, he lightly nibbled on her skin. Each thrust of his finger caused her to throw her head back against the pillow, her body arching off the mattress until she was writhing in need. His thumb brushed against her sensitive spot, and he glanced up to see her eyes shut, mouth slightly parted. "Oh God, yes..." she exclaimed, moving against his hand.

Before long, she buried her nails into his skin and cried out again. He felt her tighten around his fingers, and the sweetest sound he had ever heard filled the room as the sigh of her orgasm hit her, his name reverently slipping past her beautiful lips.

This woman was truly a marvel.

Bringing his fingers to his lips, he sucked them into his mouth, savoring her salty essence as he smiled at her. "Damn, I'd give up half my revenue to watch that on repeat," he said.

Sitting up, she brushed her hand through his hair. "That's not a very successful business model."

"Totally worth it." He kissed her forehead, resting behind her.

She reached for the waistband of his boxers and tugged, meeting his eyes. "So, is the rod in your leg the only thing that stays rigid down here?"

Without hesitation, he grabbed her by the back of the head and pulled her closer, his mouth hovering over her lips. "Why don't you touch me and find out?"

She tugged his boxers over his hips, and he assisted her in discarding them. From the look on her face, she found what she was looking for. The moment she slid her hands where he wanted her, he was rigid, ready and waiting for his own attention. With a raised brow and a grin, she lightly traced her finger along the tip of his erection before lying back on the pillow and staring up at him expectantly.

He was eager to slide into her, to feel her beneath his body, writhing, moaning, all for him.

Hovering over her, he cursed the way his hip zinged with pain and his knee ached with each bend of the mattress. He muttered curses, refusing to let the discomfort affect him. His body would need to hold out or he would find other ways to punish it later.

Reaching over to the nightstand, he grabbed a condom, tore open the packet, and rolled it on before settling between her legs. She bit her lip, watching him, the anticipation of what was about to transpire creeping into his brain. His heart was racing as he pressed against her legs. She opened further to him as he positioned himself at her slick opening, sliding slowly inside of her.

In a man's life, there are moments where the universe feels perfectly aligned. For Jackson, that was the first time he scored a touchdown at a high school football game. Riding his motorcycle up Highway 89 with the wind blowing at his back. And sinking into Allison Hanover, her fingers digging into his hips as every nerve in his body burned into oblivion.

However, this particular moment unnerved him because he had always believed that sex with a woman was simply about pleasure—get in, get off, ensure she had a good time, and move on. For him, it was that easy, and he wasn't one for repeat offenders. Once a woman left his bed, he would wash his sheets of her forever.

However, Allison felt different, and he had no idea why.

As he thrust inside her, he groaned her name as she slid her leg against his hip. He gripped her thigh, squeezing her flesh as his hips slammed against her.

"Christ," he grunted before their lips met hungrily, his tongue slipping into her mouth as he thrust inside her. Her nails pierced the flesh at his back, bucking her hips into his, sending his body into a frenzy. As if a switch had been thrown, their motions became frantic, desperate, and messy.

His knee was aching like a son of a bitch, a burn settling in his lower back. His brow furrowed in frustration. Sensing his aggravation, Allison placed her hands on his shoulders. "Why don't you let me do some of that work, big guy?" Her teeth scraped his jaw as he rolled to the side of the bed, and she crawled into his lap. Bracing his hand along her back, he held her against him as she sank down onto him.

Hissing, he ran his fingers through her hair, watching her rise and fall onto him. "Damn, you feel good," he groaned, as his fingers danced across her soft skin.

She kissed him, her arms wrapped around the back of his neck as her fingers tangled in his hair. The kiss was hard, and the desire he felt was indescribable. He lost himself in the smell and feel of Allison, buried inside of her, their tongues locked together.

With his arm bracing her back and his hand gripping her shoulder, he thrust up into her, holding her firmly against him as she cried out, her mouth open, panting, and her nails still digging into his flesh, he was sure he was going to have scratches by morning (totally worth it). "Oh God Jackson, right there, that's so good." She moaned as her chin tilted toward the ceiling with her mouth open, soft moans falling from her lips.

He felt like a damn puppy being praised by his owner. "Yeah, you like that?" He wanted to please her over and over.

As she moved her hips, he sensed he wouldn't be able to hold out much longer. He reached out, taking her hand and bringing it between them, intertwining their fingers together as they moved in motion. Their eyes made contact, and she screamed out, "Oh God," as she tightened around him. She shuddered, her face falling against his neck.

She nipped at his shoulder with her teeth, panting as her hips bucked against him and he could hold back no longer, spilling into the condom as he thrust upward into her body.

When her hips finally stilled against his, he reached up, his hand trailing with a featherlight touch against her spine, pulling her down to him and twisting her to her side, his lips pecking at her jaw as he breathed heavily into the now quiet room.

Damn, he was exhausted. He really needed to exercise more.

Her auburn hair soaked with sweat tangled and stuck to his chest. He wrapped a strand around his finger and brushed it out of her face. "If I knew it would be like that, I would've let you teach me the books sooner!" Her hand slapped at his arm as she panted against his chest. "I'll be right back," he said, pecking her forehead with his lips.

He excused himself to clean up and when he returned; she was laying back on the bed, staring at a photo on his bedside table. He climbed in beside her and pointed at the picture. "That was my mother." A woman was standing in front of a tent behind three small children, his father kneeling beside them.

"She was beautiful," she whispered.

"She was," he agreed, wrapping an arm around Allison's back and pulling her against his chest. The silence stretched for what felt like minutes while she traced small lines against the hair on his abdomen. The only sound in the room was a mix of their soft breathing as his chest rose and fell.

He felt her fingers glide along his arm before she spoke. "When did you get this?" she asked, pointing to his tattoo.

Looking down at his shoulder, he glanced at the ink. "I was eighteen, just graduated."

"A compass?" she asked, looking up at him.

"Figured it was something to remind me..." he sighed. "You know, that no matter how lost you feel, something will always guide you home."

Her fingers slid along his skin, leaving goosebumps on his flesh. "And these?" she asked.

His hand pressed on top of hers, palm resting against her hand as it sat on top of the three circles that were intertwined and engraved on his chest right above his heart. "Jackson, Dylan, Samantha," he whispered. "Three circles, never apart, always close to the heart."

"You're very close to your siblings, aren't you?"

"I'd do anything for them," he admitted.

"You're not at all what I thought you were," she whispered.

"Story of my life, Firefly," he grunted in response. "I don't think anyone has ever really taken me seriously. Hell, I had to convince my dad to sell me the shop last year. I don't even know if he thinks I can really do this. I feel like my whole life, I've just been trying to make people see me for who I am." Jax sighed and then chuckled. "I never thought I really gave a shit about all that, you know. Like who cares as long as you know who you are, but I think that's just some bullshit successful people tell themselves."

"I don't think your dad thinks you can't do this," she said.

Jax shook his head and raised her hand to his mouth to kiss her palm. "Then tell me why you're here, Allison?"

She shook her head. "He just wanted me to help you."

"Agree to disagree," he said. "Either way, you didn't think I was gonna survive either."

"I was wrong," she said, lifting her head to stare at him. "Look at everything you learned when you finally listened to me, and that was only a couple of days when you weren't being stubborn."

"Maybe I just wanted to see what was under that bra." He winked. "Sex is a great way to get my undivided attention."

"Jackson Lancaster!" Allison sat up, roughly shoving his shoulder. "You are impossible."

He shrugged and crossed his arms behind his head. "Yeah, but you still slept with me after telling me explicitly that you weren't going to tonight."

She straddled his waist and stared down at him. "Alright, well, now that I have your *undivided* attention!" She grinned devilishly. "What is COGS?"

"What?" His brow furrowed.

"Come on Jackson, you said I'd have your undivided attention. Prove it." She wrapped her hand around his once again stiffening erection, slowly pumped him in her hands. "What is COGS?"

Jackson moaned, "Cost of Goods Sold."

"Good boy," she said with a swipe of her hand over the tip. "And what are your operating expenses?"

Jax watched her in awe as she commanded him with ease, smiling at him from above. "You are a minx," he teased.

Pausing her motion with her hand, she caused him to whine, "Operating expenses! I know you know this."

"Labor supplies," he started as she began pumping him in her hand again, eliciting a loud moan from him. "Rent—Oh God!" He squeezed his eyes shut. "Accrued expenses..." His voice trailed off as she leaned over and kissed his lips.

"You've got so many more to go, Jackson. It's gonna be a long night," she teased, and Jax gripped her hips in response, bucking into her hand with a smirk.

"Bring it on!" he challenged.

Chapter Eighteen

Allison

Allison's smile lingered as Jackson kissed her lips one last time before she ducked into her car the next morning, leaving her feeling giddy and slightly off balance. She waved goodbye and then slowly drove out of her parking spot as he went into the garage.

She needed to return to her hotel, shower, and change before coming back later to go over a few more items he had questions about. In retrospect, she was sure he had just made up an excuse to see her again. She tried not to think about how adorable that was.

Jackson had surprised her. Even on the ride back to the garage this morning, he could barely keep his hands off her.

Allison wasn't sure how last night had unfolded or why it had happened.

Well, she didn't need a physical explanation. She knew how the birds and bees worked. She understood the basic laws of attraction. And Jackson Lancaster was definitely attractive. There was no point in denying it. Perhaps it was the fact that she spent so much time denying their mutual attraction that caused all the arguments and fire between them in the first place, but whatever the reason, it happened.

She had sex with Jackson Lancaster. In fact, there had been a *lot* of sex. They stayed up all night touching, exploring, kissing. Heaven have mercy, he was good in bed. But it wasn't just about the sex.

She had never been with a man who was so open and vulnerable about what he considered his shortcomings. Jackson was so concerned about his body and the way he looked after his accident. She knew he had doubts about whether his performance in bed would be good enough for her. She had never met a man so sensitive in bed yet so abrasive and difficult outside of it.

Honestly, Jackson had nothing to worry about. Sex with him had been something beyond sexual. The entire night had been a transcendent experience, unlike anything she had ever experienced before. Their connection went beyond just physical intimacy.

It was that part of it that caused her the most guilt of all.

Chip's added request for her to convince Jackson that he couldn't manage his shop was never something she took seriously. Yet she felt like she *had* tried to get in his head, to make him doubt his ability to run the shop without his brother or because of his injuries. Allison didn't know any of that for a fact. Jackson appeared capable and determined to make his shop successful, despite any challenges he might face. And Jackson really cared about his brother and would do whatever it took to help him, even if it meant finding alternate ways to run his shop.

Her guilt was eating at her and the closer she got to her hotel, the worse she felt. She knew she should just come clean and tell Jackson that her boss was interested in his shop, and that she planned to tell Chip that Jackson had declined. After all, that is exactly what had happened, minus the fact she hadn't actually told Jackson about the offer. It was only lying on a technicality, really.

However, the longer she withheld the information from Jackson, the more likely it would look like she was trying to hide something nefarious from him.

With conflicting emotions from the previous evening's euphoria and the guilt of the unspoken connection between the shop and the firm in Erie, she entered Hattie's in a distracted state. Mrs. Hattie startled her by popping out from the hallway as soon as she arrived. "There you are!"

"I'm sorry, Mrs. Hattie. Were you looking for me? I must have missed you this morning, as I left very early." Lying to an old lady was not something she wanted to do before breakfast.

Mrs. Hattie grinned at her. "Your secrets are your own, dear. But your guest was getting anxious." Allison flinched as she followed the woman's gaze toward the next room. Chip Ryder stepped into the doorway. Her heart sank at the sight of him, his smile appearing as fake as the personality he was trying to portray.

190
STACY GOFORTH

"Hello, Allie Cat. Mrs. Hattie was nice enough to keep me company while we waited for your return." His voice disoriented her.

She closed her eyes before responding through gritted teeth, "Chip, it wasn't necessary for you to come all the way down here. I told you I had everything under control."

Chip turned to Mrs. Hattie. "Isn't she adorable? My girl is always trying to take on all the stress herself."

Mrs. Hattie looked concerned. "Allison is a strong girl. I think she can handle quite a lot."

Smiling appreciatively at the old woman, Allison turned back to her boss. "Can I speak to you upstairs?" She looked at the older woman and smiled. "Sorry, we have some business to discuss."

"Of course, dear. Let me know if you need help with anything." Allison nodded at the woman before yanking Chip's arm as she pulled him toward her room.

The moment the door to her room closed, she rounded on him. "What are you doing here, Chip?"

"I thought it was important I come check on your progress." He frowned. "So, do you have good news for me, Allie, or are you sleeping with this guy just for fun?"

She felt her face drain of color as she stammered, "What—what are you talking about?"

"Seriously?" he asked, stepping toward her. "That old crow downstairs said she hadn't seen you all night. Then you come walking in here, looking like you stepped out of a Farmer's Almanac. Your hair is a wreck. Hell, Allie, you even smell like sex."

"I went out for a walk," she lied.

Chip snorted. "Where are you with the Lancaster deal?" he asked, his eyes turning dark.

"I already told you where I was." She raised her voice and looked away. "He will not sell to us. He isn't interested in giving up his shop."

"And what about all the intel I sent you? The hospital records? His brother? What did you do with that information?" he asked, searching her face for answers.

"Nothing, Chip. The information was a dead end," she groaned. "I tried. I've done everything you've asked. He's not interested in selling."

"So, what did sleeping with him have to do with anything?" he asked, stepping closer to her, backing her against the wall. "Come on Allie Cat, you're my closer. You've always got an angle." He placed his hands against the wall on either side of her body. "So, what's the angle this time?"

"There is no angle. I've done everything I can. He's not interested, Chip," she said firmly. Suddenly his mouth was on hers, his tongue penetrating her mouth with a ferocity of a man on a mission. She turned her head and shoved her hands against his chest.

"Chip, don't. I'm not in the mood," she growled.

"Wow, he was that good, huh?" he asked as she angrily stormed away from him.

Closing her eyes, she stood facing the window. "Go home, Chip."

"I'll go home when you settle the deal," he said coldly behind her. "Do I need to remind you who you work for?"

She opened her eyes and exhaled with a laugh. "I told you; he won't make the deal. He's not intimidated by Ryder Investments."

"Then maybe it's time I visited Jackson Lancaster myself, though it appears he prefers redheads," he said with a devious tone.

"No!" she shouted, spinning to face him. "Stay away from Jackson."

"Interesting," he said with a smirk. "Awfully protective of someone you barely know. That's very unlike you, Allie."

"I don't know why you are so insistent on this. I told you he's not interested." Chip walked toward her, reaching out to press one of her auburn curls behind her ear.

"Because I don't like to lose," he hissed. "I wanted that shop last year and yeah, it sucked when we didn't win the business, but then we got a second chance." His thumb slid across her cheek, causing her to stiffen. "I thought my ace analyst was going to come down here and get it for me, and I don't want to have come all this way to find out that not only will he still not sell to me, but Jackson Lancaster thinks he can steal my girl, too."

She flinched and pulled her face away from his hand. "I'm not your girl."

His palm quickly rested against her chin, fingers flailing out to grip her cheeks as he squeezed. "Allie, Allie, Allie, don't forget who you belong to," he reminded her, his voice briefly menacing before he smiled and lightly tapped her cheek with his hand. "Come now, love. Shall we get something to eat?"

She swallowed nervously as he stepped away, her heart racing. "I don't think that's a good idea. How about I go pick you up some food and I'll bring it back here?"

"Don't want your boyfriend to see me?"

"I just don't want people asking questions. It's a small town, Chip. Everyone knows everyone's business here. It's not like the city. If you start sniffing around, it's going to make things difficult." She grabbed her purse and rushed toward the door.

"Fine, but don't take too long. You know how much I hate to be locked up. This face deserves to be seen." He grinned widely as Allison opened the door and slammed it behind her, now more determined than ever to finish her business in Titusville and get out of town before her boss ruined everything.

Jackson Lancaster was a good man, and he didn't deserve whatever Chip Ryder had planned for him.

Chapter Nineteen

Jackson

J ax had the music cranked up louder than usual in the garage as he tinkered with his bike early on Friday morning. Just like the Poison song currently screaming through his speakers last night had been nothin' but a good time with Allison. He couldn't remember ever enjoying himself with a woman the way he had with her.

They had stayed up all night exploring each other in more ways than just sexually. Not that he didn't enjoy the sexual part, because hell, Allison was smoking hot, but they had spent just as much time talking as they had fucking.

After dropping her off at her car that morning, she had been all he had thought about since. It felt like a weight had been lifted off his shoulders. Even the dull ache in his hip couldn't dampen his mood. He knew it was most likely due to finally getting laid, but a part of him, maybe the part that didn't want to admit it, knew that it was more to do with Allison herself.

These were the kind of thoughts Jax wasn't ready to deal with, so he hoped to focus all of his energy on work instead. *Best laid plans*, he thought as he entered the garage that morning and found each job on his clipboard was either waiting on a part or not ready for servicing.

With nowhere else to channel his energy, he found himself where he was now; hunkered over his motorcycle, parts strewn at his feet, and for the first time in months, actual progress being made.

Despite the momentum, he noticed he was still the only one in the garage, and it was past noon. Allison still hadn't returned, and Dylan hadn't even shown up for work after last night's drunken escapades.

While he didn't expect Dylan to show first thing in the morning with what he was sure would be a killer hangover, he was tiring of being the only one who showed up for work. So, he figured a text couldn't hurt.

Jax

Yo sunshine! Killer hangover or not, the shop is still open for business!!!

Jax

You alive?

He tossed his phone onto the stool beside him and wiped the sweat off his brow before tightening the bolt on the rear suspension. Stepping back, he admired his work. "Damn fine work, Jackson!" His voice echoed through the empty garage. "Well, thank you." He chuckled. "It is a fine-looking bike, if I don't say so myself."

As his phone buzzed on the stool, he quickly reached for it.

Jax frowned, staring at the phone in his hand. What the hell was his brother talking about? Something felt off about that exchange with Dylan. Tossing his wrench to the ground, he wiped his hands on a rag and walked over to the counter. He pulled out the papers he had stored there and found Dylan's drawings stashed behind the invoices.

Thumbing through them, he was once again impressed by his brother's skill. Some drawings were simple pencil sketches, while others were more elaborate, done with markers or colored pencils. All of them exceeded his expectations of his brother's abilities.

Pausing at one drawing, he pulled it from the pile. It was a pencil drawing of a dragonfly sitting on a leaf. In the background, he recognized the tall tree with the small stone underneath it—the location he had avoided most of his life, his mother's gravestone.

Reading over his brother's texts again, he realized that Dylan's attempt at humor had inadvertently revealed his location. Dylan was at the cemetery, visiting their mother.

Jax hadn't made the trip up Church Run Road since his accident months prior. He wasn't opposed to visiting his mother, but after her passing, he found it hard to connect with her at the cemetery. To him, she existed elsewhere, so why talk to a stone?

He realized he couldn't do much more until the parts arrived, so he closed up and left a note on the door, announcing they would reopen in the morning. Climbing into his truck, he set off toward the cemetery, hoping to find his brother still there.

The drive felt ominous, each turn reminding him of the night of his fight with his dad. He had been angry and hurt, feeling betrayed that his father would consider selling the shop without consulting him. It had hurt the most that his father didn't trust him enough to even consider him as an option to run the shop in his stead.

Leaving his dad that night, he felt alone and, for the first time in his adult life, longed to be near his mother. So, he had headed for Church Run Road to talk to her, only he was so distracted with his own anger he never made it there.

Jax remembered nothing about the accident itself—not the turn in the road, not the way the bike apparently spun out, or how it hit the tree. He only remembered waking up in the hospital, feeling angry and in a lot of pain.

Perhaps it was for the best that he didn't wake up with nightmares about the crash, just the scars that served as reminders.

As he approached the familiar turn, his body tensed instinctively before his mind even registered where he was. The tree loomed into view, its bark still bearing the marks of the collision, mirroring the scars on his own body. Exhaling deeply, he pressed his foot on the accelerator and drove past, leaving the tree behind in his rearview mirror.

The cemetery turnoff was just a mile from the accident site, and soon he spotted the sign announcing its entrance. Parking his truck, he noticed Dylan's old bike near the gate. With a shake of his head, he began walking the path toward his mother's gravesite.

It didn't take long before he spotted his brother sitting on a bench near the old tree, hunched over and nursing a beer. Steeling himself for another confrontation, Jax made his presence known. "Drinking again already?"

His brother flinched, looking up with a groan. "How did you even find me? It's not like you care about visiting Mom!"

Jax was taken aback by his brother's bitter tone. "I wasn't aware you came up here either."

His brother responded sarcastically, "Every Friday, not like anyone gives a damn."

Well, this conversation was going well!

"Dylan, I don't know how to help you if you won't talk to me," he said with a sigh. "Half the time I think you don't give a shit, and the rest of the time I'm convinced you're just crying for help."

"Help from who? You?" He laughed. "Cause it sure as hell isn't Dad or Sam. And Blake pissed off so fast, it sure as hell isn't him. Seriously, fuck everyone." Dylan finished his beer and threw the bottle across the lawn like a goddamn neanderthal.

"I hope you know you're cleaning that up." He cast a warning glance in his brother's direction. "And I do not know where this attitude is coming from. Sam and Blake have always been there for you, Dyl."

"Where? I sure as hell don't see them!" he shouted. "Blake ran off to New York the moment Sam offered her bed to him."

"Oh, don't be a prick," Jax growled. "Blake fell in love with your sister, and went off to chase his dream job, and you should be goddamn happy for both of them."

"I am!" he yelled; his face red with anger. "I'm happy that they both found each other. And hooray for Blake that he figured out what he wanted to be when he grew up. But where does that leave me? Even you are leaving me behind, chasing that redhead's tail all over the garage." He reached into his backpack and pulled out another beer. But Jax was done with this self-pity bullshit. He reached for the beer and yanked it out of his hand. "What the hell, man!"

"No, you listen to me, Dylan. I'm tired of this destructive behavior. I get it, you're lonely, your best friend found happiness and left you here in town with nothing to do but sit on your hands. So, find something you want to do."

"I'm not good at anything!" he shouted.

"Bullshit. What about those drawings?" he said.

Dylan laughed. "What am I supposed to do with that? The drawings are nothing. It's bullshit. The only thing I can do with those is set them on fire to keep myself warm in the winter. Besides, my place is at the shop. That's my job, remember?"

"You hate that job. You barely even show up for it. Hell, if I was a real boss, I would have fired you already."

Dylan stood up and faced him. "Is that what this is about? Are you firing me?"

Jax sighed. "I didn't say that." He groaned and ran his palm against his face. "Dylan, you can't continue like this. Drunk and angry all the time. Last night, Allison and I had to carry you home."

"Yeah, why don't you let me worry about that," he growled.

"I can't do that," he said. "You're my brother." He put his hand on his shoulder. "Don't you get it? I love you, man. I'm worried about you. We all are. But you're my responsibility."

"Yeah, well, none of you understand me." His hands were shaking as he spoke. "No one does. I don't belong here; I don't belong anywhere. I just don't fit, Jax. I'm not like you or Sam. I don't even know who I am."

He stepped toward his brother, but Dylan backed away. "Dylan..."

"Just leave me alone, Jax." Dylan took off, running back toward his bike, leaving Jax alone under the tree.

Jax turned back toward the stone and sat down on the bench. "Well, I guess I screwed that up, huh, Ma?" Staring at her stone, he laughed. "Sorry for not visiting much, but you know I hate this stuff." He looked out over the cemetery and sighed. "Besides, the last time I tried to come up here, I crashed my bike. I'm sure you already know that."

Shaking his head, he remembered how his mother had a knack for knowing everything he ever did when she was alive. It was maddening as a young child, but when you're ten years old and lose your mother, you start missing having a mom who cared so deeply that she knew when you were about to do something stupid and talked you out of it before you screwed up. "I sure miss you, Ma. I know you would know what to do about Dyl. I'm trying my best here, but I'm feeling so lost."

He knew he could call his dad, but what was he going to do from all the way in Arizona? Sending Dylan to visit his dad felt like an option, but picturing him in an RV surrounded by senior citizens playing shuffleboard seemed more like a punishment than therapy for his brother. Besides, his dad was finally doing something for himself, and Jax felt like it was time for the siblings to rally.

"You're telling me to talk to Sam, aren't you?" he asked his mom. "She really looks after us knuckleheads in your absence. You'd be proud of her."

He dialed his sister and waited for her to answer, hoping she was already off work. Luckily, she picked up the phone on the second ring. "Hey, big bro. What's up?" she greeted cheerfully.

"Hey Sam, you busy?" he asked, trying to mask his urgency.

"I always have time for you," she reassured him.

"Thank goodness, because I need you," he admitted, sighing and sinking back against the bench.

As she exhaled, he heard the background noise change as the phone switched to speakerphone. "Sorry, just got in my car. I put you on speaker so I can drive home. New York traffic is a nightmare. So, what's going on?" she asked.

"It's Dylan, he's not getting better. He passed out drunk last night, and I found him drinking at Mom's gravesite just now," he said, closing his eyes. "She says hi, by the way. I'm here with her now." As he spoke, he smiled and gently touched his mother's gravestone.

"Aww. HI, Mom," she said, raising her voice, almost as if their mother could actually hear her—hell, maybe she could. "Okay, so, back to our irritating brother. Has he said what the issue is?"

"Honestly? He's angry at everything. You, Blake, Dad, me, hell, I think he hates the world." He laughed.

"He's mad at us for leaving him, isn't he?" she asked.

"I don't even know, honestly. He's happy about it when I press him, but when he's drunk and honest, it's all 'fuck Blake, fuck Sam.'"

"Ouch," she said. "Sorry, you've had to deal with that on your own. He's been pretty quiet with Blake and I honestly."

"I don't think he's happy here. I think he needs a break. I was thinking maybe he could come see you," he suggested nervously.

"You think he'd be agreeable to that?" she asked.

"Not if I bring it up, no," he said, letting out a loud chuckle.

"Let me talk to Blake. Maybe I can get him to invite him. But Jax, that's gonna leave you alone with the shop. Are you sure you can handle it?" she asked.

Jax stared out at the cemetery, unsure of how to answer. "I'll figure it out. I just want Dylan to be alright. That's all that matters. And I'm really worried about what's gonna happen if he keeps going like this."

"Alright, I'll talk to Blake tonight. Don't worry Jax, this isn't all on you. Let me help too." His sister's soothing voice put him at ease, and sitting at his mother's gravesite, with Sam on the phone, it was the first time in weeks that he finally felt like maybe things would be alright.

Chapter Twenty

Allison

G uilt and anxiety fueled Allison's walk to Linda's Diner, with Chip in town, causing everything to go to hell. She did not know how she was going to fix any of this, but she knew she needed to get him out of town quickly.

The bell over the diner jingled as soon as she opened the door, and the nostalgic sound of Fleetwood Mac's "Little Lies" seemed to pass judgment on her as soon as she entered. Each moment in her life always had a corresponding song, and this one felt particularly pointed. Linda recognized her immediately and waved her over. "Come on in, take a seat."

"I'm not staying today, I was just going to order for pickup." Allison hurried to the counter and sat on a stool. "Um, can I get a salad to go and maybe just a Reuben on Rye?"

"Oh, Jackson doesn't like Rye bread, you know." Linda smiled knowingly, causing Allison to frown. *These damn small towns will be the death of her.*

She sighed. "Oh, yeah, um, it's not for Jackson."

Linda seemed embarrassed before turning the order over to the line cook. "It shouldn't take long," she assured Allison. "So, um, if you don't mind my asking, how are things going over at the shop?"

Allison tried to smile, but she felt numb inside. "We've made a lot of progress. Honestly, Jackson is very smart," she said.

"He was always a very bright boy," Linda said with a glint in her eye and a telling glance. "How are you two getting along? Jamila mentioned that you both came in for dinner last night."

"We did," Allison said with a smile. "It was a late night at the shop and—"

"You don't have to explain it to me, dear," Linda interrupted, offering Allison a sense of comfort she hadn't felt all morning.

"Can I ask you a hypothetical question?" Allison asked softly.

"Of course, dear, anything," Linda said openly.

"Have you ever ... well, have you ever been less than honest with someone about your intentions, even if they were mostly innocent, hypothetically, of course?"

Biting her lip and fidgeting nervously with the hem of her shirt, Allison waited for Linda's response. "That is quite the question, Allison," Linda replied with a warm smile. "I suppose I would ask you a question as well, hypothetically." She paused. "Would this mostly innocent deception hurt the other person?"

"I don't think he would be happy to know about certain aspects of the, um, intentions," she said regretfully as the door jingled behind her.

Linda boxed up her food. "Well, dear, all I can tell you is that honesty really is the best policy." She patted her hand and smiled. "And if there was no ill intention, I'm sure he will understand."

"Who will understand what, Allie Cat?" Chip's voice behind her caused her to tense.

Squeezing her eyes shut, she turned around quickly and faced him. "I told you I would bring the food back." Looking back at Linda, she smiled nervously. "Sorry, how much do I owe you, Linda?"

"Linda, what a pretty name," Chip interrupted, stepping toward the woman at the counter. "I'm Chip."

Linda glanced at Chip with skepticism before responding. "Nice to meet you."

"Chip is my boss, and we were just leaving." She threw forty dollars onto the counter and pushed him toward the door.

"Allison, sweetie, this is way too much money. Don't you want your change?" Linda hollered after her.

"Keep it, Linda. Thanks again." Allison waved back, then angrily shoved Chip outside, staring at him with narrowed eyes. "I told you to wait at the hotel. What the hell are you doing here?"

"I just wanted to stretch my legs. I figured I would check out this town you seem to be so attached to." Chip grinned, reaching out to massage her shoulder.

She quickly shrugged him off. "This isn't a game, Chip. These are real people, with real lives, and I'm not comfortable with any of this anymore," she said, breathing erratically. When he smiled, she felt the anger swell inside of her, and she turned and stormed away from him.

Chip chased after her. "Allie Cat, what are you doing?" He grabbed her by the arm and tugged her backward. "I would strongly advise you not to walk away from me right now."

"Or what?" The fury in her eyes directed at him as she placed her finger on his chest. "Are you threatening me, Chip?"

"I'm simply reminding you of who you belong to," he growled, gripping her arm so tightly that she knew it was going to leave a bruise. "Ryder Investments owns you, I own you, and that means you do what I say."

Her nostrils flared as she stared into his dark eyes. "No one owns me, Chip. Not you, Not Ryder Investments. No one." Yanking her arm away, she stepped back. "I quit."

"You wouldn't dare." He sneered. "You'll be nothing without me, Allie. No one will hire you. I'll ruin your name."

Shoving the bag of food against his chest, she glared at him. "I'll take my chances. At least I'll still have my soul." With a smile, she turned away from him and raced toward her hotel, her heart pounding in her chest as he screamed after her.

She was terrified for her future. And she knew Chip would stick to his word and try to ruin her career. She was sure he would slut-shame her, trash her work to other investors, but she had decided she would no longer stoop to his level. Allison was done doing business with the Chip Ryders of the world.

On her way to Jackson's garage, she passed through Main Street and slowed down for a stoplight, staring over at the lease sign on the building on the corner. While sitting at the red light, she reflected on everything that had happened and the friends she had made in town.

When the light changed, she paused. Staring at the road, she realized she wanted to do something for someone else for a change. She flipped a U-turn at the light and parked her car, crossing the road. The street was exactly what you would expect from any Main Street, USA. It was quaint and friendly. The shop next door to the empty building appeared to be a small coffee shop, and across the street was a tiny bookstore.

She peered in the window of the empty store—long and narrow, with nice counter space and ample storage in the back. She jotted down the number and stored it in her pocket before being approached by a middle-aged man whose reflection she could see in the shop window. "Can I help you?" he asked.

Turning around, she introduced herself. "Oh, sorry, I'm Allison. I'm a real estate analyst. I was just taking a look at the property." Reaching into her purse, she handed him her business card.

He stared down at the card before looking up at her. "I'm Steve. This is my place. Is there something I can answer for you?" he responded hesitantly.

She paused, staring back at the window, then inhaled before letting out a soft exhale. "Actually, yes, is there a chance you're free to chat about the property?"

Chapter Twenty-One

Jackson

As the afternoon settled in, the garage seemed quieter than normal. It could have been because of the overcast sky or the fact that he had tuned the radio to an easy listening station. The current Chicago classic was creating a more casual vibe compared to his usual heavy hair band atmosphere he preferred for working. His night with Allison was definitely messing with his emotions.

He smiled as the door to the shop opened and closed, feeling anxious about seeing her again. "That must have been one hell of a shower, Firefly. I have to admit, I'm kinda jealous," he said in a flirty tone.

However, his brother's voice deadpanned across the garage, "Sorry to disappoint, but it's just me, loverboy."

"Dylan, sorry, I uh—"

Standing up from his stool, Dylan immediately interrupted, shaking his head with a smirk. "Yeah, I know what you thought."

Jax rubbed the back of his neck anxiously. "Sorry, I just haven't heard from Allison since last night and I was worried. She was supposed to stop by the garage already."

Dylan stared off toward the office. "Look, Jax, I wanted to apologize about—well, about a lot of things," he said with a chuckle. "I think I've been kinda lost lately, and I know I haven't handled things very well."

"Dylan, you don't have to apologize to me," Jax said with a shake of his head.

"Yeah, I do, man," his brother insisted, staring at the floor. "I know I haven't made it easy for you lately. I've been angry at pretty much everyone, and that's not fair." Before Jax could cut in again, Dylan continued. "Ever since Blake left, I think I kind of felt like I didn't know what I was doing with my life. Like everyone just took off and figured their shit out and here I am sitting on my thumbs. Blake fell in love and actually found something he was passionate about. And of course it was with Sam, because why wouldn't it be? I should have seen that coming years ago."

Both Jax and Dylan nodded in silent agreement. "We really should have," Jax said with a laugh before Dylan continued.

"And Sam, well, hell, I can't even be mad at her cause she deserves someone like Blake. They're disgusting together, and I think I'm jealous of that."

"So, you thought you'd find that with Donna?" Jax asked curiously.

Dylan frowned. "Hell no, I hate Donna. She's the most annoying person I've ever met. She has a hashtag for everything we do together. Did you know she even nicknamed my dick #DillPickle?"

Jax couldn't hold back his laughter. "I'm writing that down so I can text it to Sam."

"Don't you dare," Dylan warned, but then seemed to stare off as if he was trying to think of the right words. "I want what they have, though, and I'm not going to find it here."

Jax understood his brother's sentiment. There were a lot of challenges in dating in their limited social circle. Small towns weren't exactly gold mines for meeting new people.

"Even Dad is out there finding himself with the damn RV and shuffleboard, or whatever dumb thing he does now, but he's happy." Dylan was practically crying now.

"It's hard to see everyone moving on but you," Jax finished the thought for his brother when Dylan covered his face with his shirtsleeve to wipe away the dirt stained tears.

"Yeah, even you have this place," Dylan observed. "And I can see it in your eyes, Jax. You're happy here. Just being at work makes you happy." His brother shook his head. "Do you know how annoying it is to watch you work with a smile on your face when all I want to do is scream walking in the door?"

Jax watched the misery on his brother's face, pained to see him so unhappy. Being in the shop gave Jax a joy that he couldn't describe. Even when he struggled to understand the finances, coming to work was the best part of his day. Because it was something he owned, something he was making a success that had been passed down to him by his father.

"Dylan, the shop doesn't have to be your thing," he said.

"I can't leave you alone with this," Dylan said with a sob. "I'd be a terrible brother to abandon you now. Not after last year, not after..."

Jax glared at him. "Don't you dare look at me with pity, Dylan Anderson Lancaster!" His brother flinched. "I am not broken. It may take me twice as long to do an oil change as it does you, but I can still get it done. And don't you dare act like I can't hire some high school kid to come in here and help me out! But I won't have you judging me like some outsider looking in!" Dylan swallowed as Jax finished his thought. "I'm a Lancaster, we're survivors, and I can do this on my own."

"But you shouldn't have to." Dylan wiped away the tears.

"This garage is my thing, not yours. You need to go find your own thing." Walking over, Jax braced his hands on the back of Dylan's neck and leaned his forehead against his. "Whatever it takes, Dylan, I'm here for you. We're family, we support each other, and that's what I want to do. But you've done your job here. You helped me get my start, but now I need you to go."

"Are you firing me?" He laughed.

Jax inhaled. "Will it force you to leave?"

"You know I love you?" A tear ran down his cheek. "I'm just so scared."

Jax wrapped his arms around his back and hugged him tightly. "I'm your big brother. I'll always be here for you."

As they pulled away, Dylan smiled. "I think I'm gonna go visit Blake and Sam in a few months if that's okay with you." He playfully shoved Jax's shoulder. "And I'm fully aware you guys roped him into calling me to invite me out, but I think he's right. I need a new perspective."

Jax responded sheepishly, "I do not know what you're talking about, but I think it's a great idea."

Dylan shrugged and walked over to the clipboard. "Yeah whatever, I told him I wanted to make sure you have time to figure stuff out first with the garage. This is still a lot of work for one broken old dude."

"Excuse you, I'm not that old," he said with a laugh.

Dylan narrowed his eyes. "Seriously, bro, do you think you can afford to hire someone? It's not like you pay me that much."

A man cleared his voice on the other side of the garage. "Sorry to interrupt the family affair, but perhaps I could help with your little dilemma."

Jax stared at the tall man in a suit with dark brown hair standing at the entrance to his garage and noticed a candy apple red Porsche blocking his driveway. "That your car?"

The man proudly grinned. "She's a beaut, right?"

"Something wrong with it, cause it's blocking my driveway otherwise?" he asked.

The man snickered and walked toward him. "Name's Chip." He held out his hand, and Jax stared down at it. Something about this man annoyed him.

Jax hesitated for a moment, but eventually shook his hand firmly, squeezing it tighter than necessary. "Jackson Lancaster, how can I help you?"

"I think the question is, how can I help you? I couldn't avoid overhearing you talking about needing help with your shop." The man stared at him and his brother.

"You looking for a job? Gotta warn you, the pay is shit." He laughed, turning away from the man in the suit to look over his inventory.

"I'm actually here with a proposition for you." He reached into his pocket and pulled out a folded piece of paper. Jackson stepped to the other side of the counter and reached for his glasses.

Chip laid the paper on the table, and Jax picked it up and unfolded it, sliding his glasses onto his face as he looked it over, chuckling. "Is this a joke?"

The man stood taller, adjusting his suit jacket. "I can assure you, I'm quite serious. The offer on that page can be negotiated, but I don't think you'll get a better deal."

Dylan narrowed his eyes. "What's this about?" he asked.

Jackson tossed the paper back onto the counter. "I think you have the wrong place. My shop's not for sale."

"Everything is for sale; you just have to name the right price." His smarmy tone caused Jax's nostrils to flare.

"Are you deaf, Chip? I told you, shop's not for sale," he said in a much louder tone this time. "Now, if you don't mind moving that piece of junk you got there, you're blocking my driveway."

"Look Jackson, I don't think you heard me. This shop was supposed to be mine last year, but your father was a fool." Jax stared at the man, dumbfounded.

"Who the hell did you say you were again?" he asked.

"Chip Ryder, from Ryder Investments," he said, handing him a business card. "I believe you've been working with my associate this week—"

"Jackson!"

Allison stood in the garage doorframe entrance, staring at the scene in front of her. Jax tilted his head in confusion as he looked at her and then back at the asshole in the suit. "What the hell is going on, Allison?"

Chapter Twenty-Two

Allison

U pon arriving at the garage, Allison's heart sank as she noticed the red Porsche already parked haphazardly in the middle of the driveway. She realized that Chip had taken matters into his own hands by talking to Jackson before she could explain herself. She had intended to come clean about her deception and salvage whatever remained of their friendship.

But no, Chip had ruined that but coming over here to blow up anything good left in her life.

Stepping out of the car, she rushed toward the garage, eager to explain herself. The moment she entered the garage, she could hear the conversation between Chip and Jackson.

"Who the hell did you say you were again?" Jackson asked, causing Allison's heart to sink instantly.

"Chip Ryder, from Ryder Investments," Chip responded in that smug tone that Allison despised. "I believe you've been working with my associate this week—"

"Jackson!" she shouted, stepping into the doorframe, halting the conversation.

"What the hell is going on, Allison?" Jackson asked, the confusion on his face breaking her heart.

Dylan glared at her from the counter, and she swallowed the guilt she knew he must see on her face. "Jackson, I was coming over here to explain it all now."

"Explain what exactly?" he asked, looking at Chip. "Do you know this guy?"

"Chip is—" She glanced at Chip and frowned. "Chip *was* my boss."

"Your boss?" Jackson's eyebrow rose. Then he frowned, holding up the paper as he shook it at her. "You wanna tell me why he walked in here with an offer for my shop, then?"

"Jackson—" She paused, licking her lips as she tried to gather her thoughts.

"What Allie Cat is trying to say is that she should have given this to you a week ago instead of wasting your time with whatever else she's been doing," Chip interrupted, and Allison glared at him.

"Shut up, Chip!" she shouted.

Dylan threw his hands in the air. "I knew we couldn't trust you."

"Dylan, please," she begged, but he turned away from her.

Jackson's voice was harsh. "You were lying to me this whole time?" Allison felt tears welling in her eyes as she met his intense stare.

She shook her head. "I never lied to you, not really," she said. "I wasn't here for the shop. I was here to help you."

Chip interjected sarcastically, "Allie, Allie, Allie. She's good, right?" He chuckled. "This is why I pay her so well, even though she's a woman," he added. "They can be emotional to keep around, but she's so damn good to look at. Am I right?"

Jackson's anger was palpable as she watched him clench his fists at his side. "My shop isn't for sale. I'd like you both to leave."

"Please listen to me. I swear I never intended to deceive you. I just wanted to help." She begged him to listen to her, but he only turned his head away from her.

"Is that why you asked me all those questions about how I was going to manage around here on my own? Or if maybe there was something that might make me happier to do besides this? Because you were interested in taking this out from under me? Was that what last night was about, Allison? Just testing to see how broken I really was?"

Allison felt like he had slapped her. She stood in the middle of the garage with tears running down her cheeks as he stared at her with anger in his eyes.

"You really should count yourself lucky, man. She must have liked you because the bitch doesn't put out for just anyone." Chip sneered, causing Allison to gasp and cover her mouth. Before she could respond, however, Jackson's fist connected with Chip's jaw, knocking him back into the toolbox behind him.

Chip rolled around on the ground until he could stand up again, wiping the dirt off his suit. "Never call a lady a bitch," Jax grunted. "Now get the fuck out of my garage." Chip stared at him, his eyes narrowed and full of fury, but Allison knew Chip. He was a fighter in the boardroom, but a coward anywhere else.

And as expected, he backed down, turning toward her and grabbing her by the arm as he passed by. "Let's go, Allie," he growled. She stood firm in her spot on the ground. "Now," he demanded.

She turned toward him and stared into his eyes before looking down at where he had her by the arm. "Let go of me, Chip."

His grip tightened, and she winced at the pain. "Allie," he whined. "Don't embarrass me."

"I think she told you to let her go," Jackson warned. "I'd advise you to listen to her unless you're asking for more trouble."

"Are you threatening me?" Chip said, a fire burning in his eyes, yet Allison could almost smell the fear radiating off of him.

"I don't know if you know much about the Lancaster boys, but I'm not sure you're gonna like your odds of two on one," Dylan said, stepping forward.

Chip frowned and glared at her. "This isn't over Allie."

Biting her lip, she yanked her arm away. "Yes, it is, Chip." Looking back at Jackson, Chip scoffed and stomped out of the garage, slamming the door behind him.

When they were finally alone, Allison glanced up at Jackson, who refused to look at her. "Thank you," she whispered.

"Yeah, well, it wasn't about you. No man should talk about a woman that way." It shouldn't have stung so deeply, but it did.

"Jackson, I'm sorry," she said as he turned to face her. She suddenly wished he wasn't looking at her because she felt exposed and broken by the look of betrayal in his eyes. "I never meant to hurt you."

He stared at her, clenching his jaw. "So, this whole time was just about trying to get my shop?"

"No!" she said immediately. "I came here because your dad asked for help. I swear, that was it. Chip was the one who wanted the shop. I ... I should have just told him no."

"Yeah, you should have," he said coldly, breaking her heart into a million little pieces.

"I can't believe you would just lie to him like that," Dylan said.

Jax lifted his hand and pointed at his brother. "I don't need your help with this. Not now, bro."

"You have to understand. I wanted to tell you," she pleaded with both of them.

Dylan laughed. "Wanting to do something and doing them are two totally different things."

"Go somewhere else, Dyl," Jax admonished his brother. "Now."

"Fine!" Dylan growled, stomping toward the office and shutting the door loudly.

When she was alone with Jackson, she walked toward him as he immediately backed away.

"So, what was the plan, Firefly? You come here, find out how stupid I am, if my body was ready to give out or not. Check if my brother was pathetic enough to be a liability." Stepping closer to her, he leaned toward her ear and whispered, "Fuck me so I don't realize your deception," then stepped away and glared at her. "And then send your boyfriend in for the kill with a bunch of dollar signs I can't resist?"

"That wasn't it at all. I never went along with Chip's plan," she said, feeling the tears again and wiping them away immediately. "I swear to you, Jackson, I was here to help you. I never would have presented that offer to you. Chip came on his own because I was refusing to do it."

"Why stick around just to deal with my bullshit all week?" he asked. "What was last night? Why Allison? What was the point of that?" he shouted, his voice echoing so loudly in the garage it caused her to flinch.

"Because I care about you!" she yelled, surprising herself. "Dammit, I didn't mean for it to happen. You're an asshole, but I care about you, Jackson."

He looked away from her, muttering, "Bullshit."

"I had planned to leave on the first day, but your dad convinced me to stay because I felt needed for once. No one has ever needed me before." She reached for him, but he pulled his hand away. "You refused help every single day, but I knew you wanted it. I could sense it behind all that stubbornness you showed. There's something about you, Jackson, that I can't explain, but I'm drawn to you."

"Then un-draw it, Allison. Go home. I don't want to see you ever again." His voice was hoarse and dark. She had never seen him so serious.

"Jackson, you don't mean that," she pleaded. "I know you felt it, too. Last night was special. There's something between us that even you can't explain."

He turned his head and moved away from her. "Last night was just sex. That's all."

"Jackson..." she sobbed.

"Go back to Erie, Allie Cat," he growled, as the name rolled angrily off his tongue. She watched sadly, tears streaming down her face, as he walked toward his office and exited her life.

Chapter Twenty-Three

Jackson

Jax could not focus after watching Chip and Allison leave. Overwhelmed by anger, he watched as Dylan stood up and faced him when the office door slammed shut. "Is she gone?" Dylan asked.

Jax scowled. "Don't act so goddamned happy about it."

"Bro, I'm not happy to be right, but I sensed something was off about her—"

"Enough, Dyl. I don't want to hear it!" Jax yelled.

Dylan flinched and settled back into his chair. "Fine, but try to see this as a positive, Jax. At least now you know the truth."

"Positive?" Jax snapped at Dylan. "Can't you see? None of this is positive, alright?"

Dylan shrugged. "She deceived you, and now you're aware. I mean, it's not like you actually liked this girl, anyway." Jax winced and glared at his brother. "Wait, Jax, did you actually..."

"I need to leave." Jax turned and stormed out of the office, leaving Dylan shouting behind him.

The moment he got to the front door of the garage, he paused as he heard voices. Peering into the darkness, he witnessed Allison and Chip arguing by Chip's ugly ass sports car. "You can't resign, Allie Cat!" Chip yelled as Allison walked toward her car.

"I already have, three hours ago," she said. "I never enjoyed working for you, anyway."

"Who will complete the Sanderson deal?" Chip whined.

She turned back to him, her cheeks flushed red with anger. "You handed that deal to Larry. I worked hard for it, did things I regret because of you, and you just gave it to Larry to manipulate me into things I didn't want to do." Approaching Chip, she placed her hand on his chest. "I didn't want any of this. I came here to assist a friend of the family, and you made it ugly. You did this."

"Don't act all superior now, Allie Cat. You've always handled your own dirty business without my help," the man said scornfully.

"I'm done, Chip. I'm not proud of who I am anymore." Jax watched as Allison's face crumbled and tears welled in her eyes. He was so angry with her, so conflicted about her betrayal, that he didn't know how to feel watching her now. "One day, I have to learn to be okay with who I've become. I don't know how to do that yet, but somehow, I'm going to have to learn to live with that. But what I do know is that I want nothing to do with you anymore."

"You won't make it without me." Chip sneered.

Allison chuckled. "Maybe, maybe not. But I'm willing to take that chance and find out." She turned away from him.

"You slut!" Chip growled. Jax's hand moved toward the door just as Allison turned back, advancing toward Chip. "When I found you, you were worthless. I made you."

Allison confronted him by his car, her hand connecting with his cheek, the sound reverberating through the parking lot. "I eat men like you for breakfast, Chip." Jax couldn't stop the smile from forming across his lips. "I was strong the day I met you, but I'm even stronger walking away," Chip grunted, heading to his car.

Allison walked to her car, glancing back. "Oh, and Chip?" Chip turned to face her. "I faked every orgasm I ever had with you. It actually dawned on me after last night, just how shit you actually were in bed." With a shrug, she got in her car and drove off.

Despite his anger at the entire situation and at Allison specifically, he found their exchange oddly gratifying.

After an hour, Jax found himself unable to remain at the garage. He needed to talk to someone who would understand and be supportive, and Dylan didn't fit the bill. Jax entered the diner and quickly made his way to a corner booth, trying to avoid drawing too much attention. He sank into his seat, gazing at the menu, immediately regretting his decision to come here. But as soon as Mrs. F cleared her throat, he instantly knew he had made the right choice.

"Hey, Mrs. F," he greeted with a mix of friendliness and sadness.

"I had a feeling I might run into you," she said, sliding into the booth opposite him. A mother's intuition is a powerful thing, even when she's not your biological mother. Jax rarely confided in Linda Forrester, but when he was feeling low, she was the one he turned to. "I had a rather unpleasant encounter with a man named Chip today. Is that why you're here, sulking in my diner tonight?" she asked.

"She lied to me," he said, his voice shaky as he struggled to control his emotions.

"Did she explain why?" Mrs. F asked, surprising Jax with her question. It was as if she already knew exactly who and what he was talking about.

"It doesn't matter why she lied," he said, snorting out his frustration.

Reaching out across the table, Mrs. F placed her hand over his. "Jax, honey, I doubt Allison intended to deceive you."

Jax glared out the window. "Doesn't matter what her intentions were, she had the chance to tell me the truth, and she chose not to. It's pretty straightforward," he argued.

Linda sighed. "I'm not sure of the details, and you don't have to share them with me. But when she spoke to me, she was genuinely remorseful and wanted to talk to you."

"Well, she didn't. Instead, her boyfriend or boss, whoever he was, did it for her," Jax growled in frustration.

"Oh, dear," Linda said, a soft sigh exiting her mouth as she sank into the booth.

"I thought she wanted to help me, Mrs. F. But really, all she wanted was my damn shop. She wasn't interested in me at all," Jax said. Disappointed, he realized that what bothered him the most was that Allison had no genuine interest in *him*, Jackson Lancaster. The reality was that everything that happened this last week had nothing to do with him at all.

"Are you upset because she lied, or because you truly cared for her and are disappointed that she may not have cared for you in return?" Linda asked, squeezing his hand.

"I just thought for once someone saw me, you know? Actually, saw me, scars and all." His voice shook as his feelings overwhelmed him. The tears fell, and Jax finally let the emotions of the day defeat him, slumping into the booth as he sobbed.

Lost in his sorrow, Jax didn't even notice when Mrs. F slid into the booth beside him, enveloping him in a comforting embrace. He leaned into her, allowing his emotions to wash over him completely.

Chapter Twenty-Four

Allison

After leaving the garage, Allison knew she needed to leave town. Standing in the middle of her room, she angrily threw her clothes into her suitcase as tears dried on her cheeks. It had been one of the worst days of her life. Losing her job, damaging her reputation at a big investment firm, and worst of all, ruining things with Jackson—it was all a mess.

Her career she could salvage; she was smart, excelled at her job, and knew all the skeletons in Ryder Investment's closet. That was called leverage, boys and girls. She would dig her career out of the dumpster fire it was currently in. Even if it took her a while to get there.

The destruction of her relationship with Jackson was another story altogether, even though they didn't really have a relationship.

They had only known each other for a little over a week, so it was more of a fling than anything else. Despite this, she couldn't deny the strong connection she felt with him, a connection that she couldn't quite understand.

But last night was special to her. Being with Jackson felt different from any other man she had slept with. It was more than just sex. It was more than just a physical connection; it was something deeper and inexplicable.

However, she had sabotaged that connection with her lies and deceit. She realized she should have been honest with him at the cabin, especially about her ties to Ryder Investments and Chip's interest in his shop.

In hindsight, she saw many things she could have done differently, but now she had to face the consequences. It seemed that one of those consequences was losing the opportunity to explore whatever connection existed between her and Jackson.

She dragged her suitcase across the floor and left her room, heading toward the front of the house. "Allison? Are you leaving tonight?" Mrs. Hattie stood in the living room, staring at her.

"Indeed, ma'am. It's time for me to head back to Erie," she said as she set her suitcase against the door before walking over to the woman. "I just want you to know that I truly appreciate everything you've done for me and all the kindness you've shown me."

"I've simply enjoyed finally having someone in my home," the woman said with a warm smile. "If you're ever in town again, you know where to stay."

"Actually, Mrs. Hattie, I was thinking about that," she said. "Have you thought about marketing?"

"Marketing for what, dear?" Mrs. Hattie asked.

"This house is historical. I'm certain that it could draw people in if you advertised it correctly. Online marketing could reach the right customers and bring them to town," she suggested, pulling up her phone to show Mrs. Hattie some examples of other historical sites in neighboring towns that were successful in attracting visitors.

"That's wonderful, and it sounds amazing, but I wouldn't know the first thing about running something like that," Mrs. Hattie admitted.

"That's where I come in." She smiled. "Turns out I'm going to have a bit of free time on my hands, so maybe I can help you out by setting some of the initial stuff up."

"You'd do that for me?" Mrs. Hattie asked.

"Of course I would. You've been so gracious to me, I'm happy to return the favor," she said, hugging her before stepping back. "I'll be in touch, alright."

"Take care of yourself, Allison," the woman said with a smile, taking her by the hand and gripping her. "Remember, when the roots are strong, love can withstand any storm." Allison gasped quietly, biting back a sob. Mrs. Hattie was a sweet old woman, but love? No, whatever it was between her and Jackson, the storm had already come and swept them away.

She shook her head and smiled at her. "You take care, Mrs. Hattie."

Twenty minutes later, Jamila greeted Allison upon her arrival at the diner. "Girl, I heard I missed all kinds of drama this morning."

Allison frowned. "News sure travels fast in a small town."

"Hell, yeah it does. Did your boss really show up here and blow everything up?" Jamila asked with a concerning glance.

"Blew them sky high and then set the remains on fire." She laughed with a slow head nod.

"You wanna talk about it?" she asked. "We could grab a drink at Boondocks." The last thing she needed was another pity party.

"I'm actually heading back home to Erie." She looked back toward her car parked out front of the diner. "But I wanted to leave you with this." She pushed a folder across the counter toward her.

"What's this?" she asked.

"I went by that shop on the corner of Main." Jamila's eyes went wide. "I know you said you didn't want my help, but I was curious about it, and you know what they say about curiosity and the Allie Cat." She grinned.

"What did you do?" Jamila asked.

"The owner, Steve, is actually waiting for a call from you. He's very interested in your offer." Allison smiled, and Jamila stared back at her with a bewildered look. "You know, the very reasonable offer that you were prepared to make earlier."

"Are you serious?" she squealed and wrapped her arms around her in a hug. "Oh my God, Allison, I can't believe this. Now you have to come to Boondocks with me to celebrate. You can have a coke while I get drunk." She giggled.

Allison couldn't help but feel excited for her friend and realized she wanted to stay and celebrate with her. Erie could wait a couple more hours. "Alright, one drink."

Boondocks was busier on Friday night compared to the last time she had been there. The country music was blasting, and couples were on the floor dancing to a Mauren Morris song. "So, you wanna tell me what happened?" Jamila asked as she sipped her cocktail.

Allison stared at the table in front of her, picking at the chipped acrylic with her fingernails. "I came here to help Jackson, just like I said I did, but my boss had ulterior motives about buying his shop ... and I failed to mention that to Jackson until Chip showed up with an offer today."

"Ouch," Jamila said. "I'm guessing he's butthurt now."

"He's furious, and it really didn't help after last night." She frowned, glancing up to meet her friend's eyes.

Jamila narrowed her eyes and licked her lips. "Okay, now you have to dish, because last night the two of you looked like you were about to eat each other up."

"I can't even describe it," she sighed. "It was—"

"Girl, you are blushing hotter than a chili pepper," she teased. "I can't believe it! You and Jackson, after all that denying it. So, how good is he?"

"It was the best night of my life," she admitted. "And now, now I don't know what to do. He won't even look at me without this anger in his eyes." Her heart sank back down to her toes, a sadness she didn't even realize she could feel was now apparently taking up permanent residence in the pit of her stomach.

"Are you sure you don't want a drink?" Jamila asked with a frown. "I think you deserve one after this week."

Allison sighed. "Maybe just one."

"Your wish is my command." Jamila jumped up and took off to the bar.

Allison sat in the booth, tapping her fingers against the wooden table anxiously. Maybe the feeling of home and Erie would allow the sadness to subside. She could curl up under her blankets, plug into her music and let the world disappear. After a few days, all this melancholy and the Jackson of it all would be something she would just forget.

Suddenly, Dylan appeared beside her. "Can I ask you something?"

Startled by his appearance, she hesitated. "Dylan—of course. Have a seat." She gestured to the booth across from her that Jamila had just vacated.

"Why'd you do it?" he asked. "Why'd you lie to my brother?"

Allison sighed. Today really wasn't her day. "Dylan, it's not that simple," she began, knowing there wasn't much she could say to Dylan that he would believe. "I swear to you I didn't come here trying to deceive Jackson."

"How am I supposed to trust that?" he asked skeptically.

"If I wanted his shop, I would have pushed for it. Believe me, I'm good at my job," she added with a laugh. "I had enough intel to use against him and I chose not to use it, because his shop wasn't of any interest to me."

"So, what did you come for?" Dylan demanded.

"I came because your dad asked me to," she answered, and it was an honest response. She wouldn't have come if Ken hadn't called her. "Our parents were close friends in high school. I did it as a favor to him."

"Alright, and after Jax acted like an ass, after all the shit he pulled, why did you stay?" he asked further, settling back in his seat and studying her.

She sighed. "I know you don't believe me, but I care about Jackson." She shook her head and bit her lip. "Your brother might be an asshole, but I've never met anyone like him. He's pigheaded, resilient, and has the most stubborn determination I've ever seen in a man."

"Yeah, he kinda sucks." Dylan laughed. "You mind me asking something else?"

"Might as well. I have nothing to hide from you." She shrugged.

"What kind of intel did you have on him?" She had expected this question from Dylan.

"Chip sent me Jackson's medical records, so I knew the full extent of his injuries and the limitations of what he could manage at the shop on his own."

Dylan nodded, processing the information. "On his own..."

"Well, he also sent me some intel on you," she admitted hesitantly. "He thought it might help show that you weren't exactly reliable help around the shop."

"Because of my drinking?" he asked.

"I don't know, I guess. It was an article about a fight you had here with your friend and a baseball player last year."

Dylan stared at her with a smirk on his face. "That fight was about my sister. Blake and I were defending her honor from a complete and total jackass."

"Well, either way, I didn't use any of it against Jackson. I asked him a couple of questions, but that's all," she said. "I know you don't trust me, but all I care about is what is best for your brother."

"Then, perhaps you and I finally found something we have in common, Allison," Dylan said casually as he rose from the table.

"Can you do me a favor?" she requested before he left. "Can you tell him something for me?" He nodded in agreement. "Can you tell him it's not just a compass that can guide you home? Sometimes you have to follow your heart."

Chapter Twenty-Five

Jackson

J ax had spent the last hour working on his bike, trying to get the thoughts of Allison out of his head. She had said that she didn't lie to him, but how could he believe that when she had spent so much time asking him questions about his life, talking about his injuries, pretending to care about Dylan and his issues? He didn't know what to believe anymore.

The wrench slipped from Jax's hand as he tried to tighten the seat post bolt one more time on his bike. "Dammit!" He tossed the wrench to the ground and stepped away from the bike.

"Hey now, you're almost done with it. Don't break it now." Dylan stood with a smirk on his face behind him.

"I thought you went out for the night?" Jax asked in irritation.

"I did," he said slowly, walking over to the counter. "I uh, I ran into Allison."

"Man, you couldn't have been more right about that one, huh?" Jax said with a shake of his head. "I should have listened to you when you told me not to trust her."

Dylan laughed. "Hell, no one should listen to me. I've been drunk for weeks. I don't know what I'm talking about half the time."

"What do you mean? You were right about her the whole time," Jax said.

"I'm paranoid by nature, Jax. I don't trust anyone." His brother shrugged. "Doesn't mean I'm right."

"Well, doesn't mean you're wrong either," Jax grunted.

"Dammit, Jax, stop being so damn stubborn for once in your life!" Dylan yelled. "You care about her, don't you?"

Jax stared at the ground. "I thought I did, but—" Jax cursed under his breath. "I don't know what I feel."

"Bullshit, Jax. I know you. I've never seen you like this before." Dylan shook his head. "Not over a chick, man. You've never cared about a girl like this. You've never even wanted to sleep with a woman more than once, and I saw you this afternoon when you thought I was her. You were looking forward to seeing her again."

"That means nothing!" Jax protested, not wanting to hear what his brother was saying. "I don't even know if anything she said to me was real."

"I think it was," Dylan mumbled. "I think she cares about you. But I don't think you should listen to what I, or Chip, or anyone else says about her. Only you and Allison can know what your truth really is."

"I don't know how to find that truth." Jax shook his head in a state of despair.

"Talk to Allison." Dylan shrugged.

"She went back to Erie." He laughed. "You know, I guess it was fate that I never even got her phone number."

"You know what I always say?" Dylan offered with a smile. "There is nothing a visit to Boondocks can't fix."

"Dylan, I know we just talked about you finding a new perspective, so this seems like a pretty bad time for you to suggest I go get sauced." He laughed.

"Tonight, someone told me to tell you it's not just a compass that can guide you home. Sometimes you just have to follow your heart," Dylan leaned against the counter.

Jax sat up on his stool and stared back at him, his heart pounding in his chest. "I, uh..."

"Like I said, Boondocks seems like the place to be tonight." Dylan turned with a shrug and walked out of the garage.

Jax drove his truck through town toward his cabin, contemplating his brother's words the entire drive home. He had not expected Dylan to come to Allison's defense, considering he had been so distrustful of her the entire time. But he had talked to her and changed his mind, and maybe that meant Jax should too, but something was holding him back from doing that—being stubborn will do that.

As his phone rang, he answered it and heard his dad's voice come through the line. "Hey, son, I didn't interrupt you, did I?"

"Ain't got much else to do on a Friday night, Dad." He laughed sarcastically, turning onto Main Street as the light turned green.

His dad's easy chuckle momentarily set him at ease until he spoke. "Good, good. I just felt like I should check up on you. See how things were going with the shop? Did things work out with Allison?" Suddenly, his thoughts were on Allison. He knew his dad meant the finances, but that was the farthest thing from his mind.

"I uh, yeah, Dad, the finances are all figured out," he answered after a brief silence.

"Everything alright there?" his dad asked. "You seem off, Jax."

"Can I ask you something?" he asked, and his dad grunted his approval. "It's about last year, when you were trying to sell the shop to Ryder Investments."

"Ah." There was a long pause. "Yeah, what about it?"

"Allison was involved in the proposal for the shop, right?" he asked.

His dad chuckled. "She was. She came out and did the appraisal, checked the place out, did the workup and gave me the offer."

"So, you were aware how badly she wanted to buy this place, and you still sent her down here?" he said with a grunt.

"Allison doesn't want your shop, Jax." His dad sighed. "After I told her I was selling it to you, sure she told me I would make more money on their deal, but I never heard from her again." He paused. "Her boss is a different story. I think I got about ten offer letters from him until I just started having them returned to sender."

"Yeah, Chip's a real winner," Jax grumbled.

"Anyway, Allison and I have had no contact until I called her last week and asked her to come down and help you," his dad said in his usual chipper tone.

"I'm sure she jumped at that enormous opportunity for a payday," he said sarcastically.

His dad sighed. "Actually, son, she tried to turn me down multiple times."

"What?" Jax was clearly surprised by this news.

"Yeah, she told me no, said she was busy, too much on her plate. You name it, and that girl had an excuse for it. She had no interest, but she finally agreed to come down when I told her you needed her. I might have talked to her mom and thrown in a little nostalgic guilt tripping."

Jax felt confused. If Allison really didn't want to come down to his shop, then maybe she was being honest about not being involved in Chip's interests, after all.

The storm that had been threatening all day finally unleashed above him, as raindrops fell on his windshield.

"Look, Jax, I don't know exactly what's going on down there, but if you think that girl came there to deceive you, she didn't. Allison is a good girl. She was doing me a favor. I know you don't trust outsiders, kid..." Staring at the rain-soaked windshield, Jax closed his eyes at the traffic light. "Sometimes you gotta learn to let people in."

A car honked behind him, and he opened his eyes to the green light over his head. Suddenly, he knew what he had to do.

"Dad, I gotta go."

Chapter Twenty-Six

Allison

Allison hugged Jamila goodbye and promised to contact her on Monday morning to help with the negotiations on the nail shop lease. Allison was thrilled about her friend's new adventure and promised to drive back down to be her first customer.

Back in Erie, Allison hadn't had any female friends since college. It was one sacrifice she had made by living in a male-dominated world. But since coming to Titusville, Jamila had been kind and respectful to her. Allison felt proud to have done something for Jamila without the expectation of personal gain. It was a feeling she hadn't had in years.

As she looked around the old bar, she realized she was actually going to miss Titusville. The small town initially felt intrusive and suffocating, but the people welcomed her with open arms.

"You stay safe out there, ma'am!" Rusty, the rugged bar tender with a permanent scowl but a heart of gold, called out to her as she walked to the door. "I think it's finally decided to rain tonight."

"Thanks!" she replied politely as she opened the door and stepped out into the night.

The rain felt almost cathartic as it washed over her, drenching her hair and face immediately. Hurrying to her car, she unlocked the door and sat in the driver's seat. The raindrops drummed relentlessly on the glass. Allison brushed her wet hair away from her face, closed her eyes, and sat in the darkness.

Everything had gone wrong since she had arrived in Titusville. She groaned but corrected herself. Jackson Lancaster felt right. Meeting Jackson had been one of the best thing to happen in her life in a long time. He was challenging, stubborn, kind, and funny. He pushed her in a way no one else ever had. She fought back tears, wiping her face. "Pull it together, Allison."

She pushed the button to start her car, only to be greeted by the unpleasant sound of her car grinding. "What the hell?" She tried again, frowning. "Please, not now!" Popping the hood, she got out of the car and hurried to the front, peering into the complex engine components she couldn't even recognize. "Ugh!" she growled as the rain kept relentlessly pouring down on her.

"Car trouble?" A voice behind her made her turn. Jackson stood there in the rain, his white shirt drenched, hair sticking to his forehead. "I know a mechanic who could help you with that."

"Jackson..." Her voice got drowned out by the rain. "What are you doing here?"

"I can't get you out of my mind, Allison," he confessed, his voice breaking. "The day you walked into my garage with those goddamn heels and that stick up your ass, I swear to God, you're the most annoying woman I've ever met in my entire life." He sighed as he approached her. "You can't drink without making that ridiculous face. You don't even know the difference between a wrench and a screwdriver. Hell, you get in the goddamn way every single time you walk in the garage." He took another step toward her, shaking his head. "But if I just let you walk away now, I'm gonna regret it for the rest of my life."

Tears mixed with rain streamed down her face. "You and I would never work," she argued, more to herself than to him.

He smiled, rainwater running over his face and lips. "Maybe not." Standing in front of her, he reached out and touched her cheek. "But my heart led me here to you, so I thought maybe that meant something."

His thumb brushed across her bottom lip, igniting a firestorm inside of her. Without hesitation, she wrapped her arms around his neck, her lips crashing against him, moaning the moment they touched. His hand gripped her waist, pressing her against the car. Allison felt dizzy with emotion, completely drunk on desire. But all she saw was Jackson. All she needed was Jackson.

Running her hand along his jaw, she kissed him deeply, her fingers tangling in his wet hair. "I couldn't just let you leave," he whispered in her ear, his hand sliding up her skirt, leaving a trail of heat against her skin.

"I didn't want to leave," she moaned softly into his neck, her tongue caressing his wet skin. She felt a surge of wild abandon she couldn't explain. The door to the bar opened, and Jackson stopped, pulling her close as the sounds of people chatting drifted across the parking lot.

"Jackson..." She gazed up at him, breathing heavily as their bodies pressed together, feeling his arousal against her leg.

He took her hand and led her silently through the parking lot until they reached the back of the bar. In the dim alley, he pulled her toward him, and their lips met in a passionate kiss. "Allison..." he murmured against her lips.

She felt like a teenager, sneaking away to make out under the bleachers. It was reckless, irresponsible, and oh, so very hot.

Reaching between them, she touched the bulge growing in Jackson's pants beneath the damp fabric. He groaned into her rain-soaked hair. "Damn, you make me crazy. I can't explain it. I feel like I'm eighteen again." He chuckled.

"Ever done it in an alley before?" she teased, slipping her panties off and flashing a mischievous grin. He shook his head no, but then gaped at her.

"What are you doing, Firefly?" he asked in surprise, his head falling back against the wall as she touched him again. "I don't have anything on me," he said in frustration.

Unbuttoning his pants, she nibbled at his jaw. "It's okay, I'm on the pill."

"Are you sure, Allison? We don't—"

"Jackson, I've spent all day thinking I lost you. I don't want to wait another minute." His eyes met hers and the intensity of his stare caught her off guard. He grabbed the back of her head, spun her around so her back was against the wall, and kissed her furiously. His other hand slid along her thigh, sliding it under her dress until she felt his fingers slip inside her, moving in and out of her ever so slowly, as she rocked against his hand, moaning softly.

Opening her eyes, she found him watching her. His eyes burned into her in the dark. His teeth bit against the flesh of his lips as he concentrated on his task, so determined to bring her pleasure that Allison lost herself in her own satisfaction. It was his smile that sent her over the edge, the way he so smugly had her crying out his name. She couldn't resist this man, not for anything.

They both reached for his zipper, fumbling together in the dark to free him from his constraints. After a few stumbles and a couple curses as he tried to find the right position, Jackson lifted her against the wall and swiftly entered her with a grunt. Their mouths met, silencing her loud curse and the scream she wanted to release into the rain-soaked night sky.

This encounter differed from the one in the cabin. It was primal, carnal, a sensation that began with her skin prickling and culminated in a fire burning so deep that only the erratic pounding from Jackson thrusting inside of her could extinguish it.

Allison had never felt so undone in her entire life. She never expected that sex in an alleyway would be one of the most transformative experiences of her life. Yet here she was, being taken apart with each thrust and fused together with every frantic kiss Jackson planted on her lips.

Her body erupted, unable to contain itself any longer, and Jackson tightly gripped her hip as he thrust upward with a grunt, whispering her name in her ear.

Rain continued to fall on them as they stood there, chests heaving, staring at each other. They both laughed nervously, and Jackson stepped back, readjusting his jeans before turning to her, water dripping from his face. Allison brushed the hair away from his forehead and lightly kissed his lips. His arms enveloped her in a gentle embrace, a stark contrast to their recent intensity against the wall. "You'll catch a cold out here," he murmured against her lips. "Come home with me."

Her fingers clenched his wet shirt. "Not like I can leave you. My car won't start," she said with a smirk, biting her lip.

"What a shame," he teased, intertwining their fingers and leading her softly toward his truck. "Come on, let's get you dry, and we can talk at home."

Home, she thought. She liked the sound of that.

Epilogue

Jackson

Four months later...

Jackson sat at the kitchen table reading an article on his phone titled "How to Increase Revenue: 13 Strategies." Because that's who he was now, a legitimate businessman, dedicated to reading articles and implementing strategies to enhance their business ventures. Or at least that's what he told his girlfriend. Glancing through the article, he gently put his phone down and patted his dog on the head as he entered the room with excitement. "Okay boy, calm down. We're leaving shortly."

Allison padded into the room, her hair in a messy bun, yawning. "Is Dylan here yet?" She opened the fridge and pulled out the bag of kale Jax hated more than anything in the world. Standing up, he embraced her from behind, burying his face in her shoulder.

"Morning, Firefly," he whispered, showering her neck with kisses, making her giggle and lean into him.

"Hey, we're gonna be late," she scolded, tossing the kale onto the counter and turning to kiss him.

Jackson 1, Kale 0.

"We own the place. We can be late if we want to be," he teased, letting his tongue slide into her mouth.

"Jackson," she whined. "It's a poor business model."

"Yes, but it's very good for my dick, babe," he said.

Just then, the front door opened, and Dylan greeted them. "Hey! Shit, should I close my eyes? I'm still not over last week."

Allison laughed and pushed Jax away. "We're decent ... this time."

"I hope to hell that Sam and Blake aren't like this in New York. I saw enough of them when they first got together," Dylan groaned, taking a seat at the kitchen table. "But you two are impossible. No place is sacred."

Jax winked at Allison and playfully smacked her bottom. "Are you all packed?" he asked, turning his attention to his brother.

"Yeah, suitcase packed, bus ticket ready. New York City, here I come," Dylan said. "I can't believe I'm going to get to be in the city for Christmas."

"Make sure to visit Rockefeller Center and see that gigantic tree," Jax said. "But don't pull a 'Home Alone' while you're there. Your sister doesn't need her place messed up."

"Dude, you realize I'm a fucking adult, right?" Dylan asked sarcastically.

"Prove it," Jax said as he playfully tousled his brother's hair. Allison started the blender. Her kale smoothie turned an unappealing shade of green, as it blended down into a disgusting mixture that Jax still refused to drink. "Alright, what time does your bus leave?"

Dylan checked his phone. "Forty-five minutes. I should head out," he announced, getting up just as Allison finished pouring out her smoothie.

"Here, take this." Allison handed him a brown paper sack.

Dylan eyed it suspiciously. "There's nothing healthy in here, is there?"

Allison chuckled. "Absolutely not, nothing but the worst snacks possible for my favorite Lancaster."

She hugged him tightly as Jax protested, "I thought I was your favorite?" Allison shook her head, returning to her meal prep. "Come on, I'll walk you out." He gestured to his brother, following him to the door.

"You guys sure you'll be alright at the shop?" Dylan worried once they were alone outside on the porch. "Will is pretty slow with the oil changes, and I know Allison is taking over all the books and stuff, but..."

"Dylan, we're fine," Jax said, reassuring his little brother. "What about you? You gonna be alright?"

"Yeah, I'm good. Looking forward to seeing some new scenery." He laughed.

"Maybe a few new women?" Jax asked. "How did Donna handle the news?"

Dylan rolled his eyes. "I think she was more pissed off that I'm getting to go see Blake and she isn't." He shrugged. "Donna was never a thing for me."

Jax patted his back. "Good, go find your happy, bro."

Dylan shook his head and wrapped his arms around his waist. "I'm gonna miss you, bro." Jax cupped his hand around the back of Dylan's head and squeezed an arm around his back.

"I'll miss you too," he said, realizing that he meant it more than he cared to admit. "Don't forget to let some light in to those dark places you hide in now and then, alright?" he whispered, patting him on the back.

"I'll try," he heard his brother mumble into his chest. "I'll call when I get there."

Dylan pulled away, rushing off the porch, turning to wave as he jogged down the path toward the main house. Jax watched him go, feeling a pang of sadness. Behind him, the front door opened as Allison joined him on the porch. "You alright?"

Jax chuckled. "Not really, but I will be."

"He's gonna be fine," Allison reassured gently, wrapping her arms around his waist.

Jax sighed. "I know. I did my best. I just hope Sam's ready for him."

"Where did you put the folder I had on the desk for Jamila?" Jax looked up as Allison entered the garage from the office. He and Will, his newest mechanic, were finishing the inventory for the day's work.

"Sorry, I moved it to the file cabinet. Didn't want it to get lost in next month's revenue report," Jax said, wiping his brow with a rag and smiling at Allison, who stood with her arms crossed at the counter. "What?" he asked, feeling her eyes trail over him.

Allison shrugged. "Nothing, you just look hot, covered in grease."

"We can't scandalize Will yet." Jax gestured to Will, who was working on a Ford Bronco. "Dylan's rules. At least not until he's past his first ninety days."

"You act like I don't have any self-control." She grinned.

Jax walked over, smirking, and kissed her cheek. Leaning over, he whispered in her ear, "I know for a fact you don't."

She giggled as he kissed her neck. "Jackson, stop it."

Startled, Will looked up from the engine. "Sorry, kid!" Stepping back, he shot her a serious glance. "You need to behave, Allison."

"Know anyone who can look at an RV around here?" A booming voice at the front door made Jax's heart soar.

He turned, surprised. "Dad?"

"I heard I could get a good deal if I stopped by." His dad smiled and walked toward him, gripping him tightly in a hug that Jax had missed more than anything.

"What are you doing here? You just missed Dylan. He left for New York a couple of hours ago." Jax stared at his father in shock.

His dad laughed. "Yeah, I know. Your sister told me. I'm actually heading to New York next. But I wanted to check in here first, see how the two of you are treating the old shop." His dad looked around, nodding appreciatively. "Looks good, Jackson. You do not know how proud it makes me to see what you've done with the place."

A warmth spread through Jax's chest at the comment, making it hard to hide the joy blooming on his lips. His father's genuine approval meant the world to him.

"Allison keeps me in line," Jax said, smiling, pulling her close.

His father chuckled. "That I do not doubt at all. Come here, kiddo." He turned toward Allison with a huge smile. It seemed unfair how quickly Allison had garnered his dad's favor. Half the time, Jax was sure his dad enjoyed phone conversations more with her than him, though perhaps it was because of the hours of advice that Allison gave him about women.

Allison hugged his father. "Hello, Ken. I wish you had told us you were stopping by. How long will you be in town?"

"Couple of days, then I'm gonna go see Sam and Blake, and I guess Dylan now," he said with a grin. "But first, I'm heading to Linda's Diner to check on her. I heard she had to hire another waitress because of you," he added, chuckling as he glanced at Allison.

"I felt guilty at first, but Jamila's new nail shop is really popular in town. She's thriving, and the new waitress is bringing in a lot of business for the diner. Her photos are all the rage on Instagram." Allison shrugged, Jax simply grumbling in annoyance.

"Just what we needed—#blessed at Linda's Diner," he said, earning a playful smack on the shoulder from Allison.

"You should be nicer. Everyone needs a job. Donna was humble about needing one, and Linda was kind enough to hire her," Allison pointed out.

Jax grumbled, "I still think she's trouble."

His father chimed in. "You think everyone is trouble, Jackson! Well, I'm gonna head over to the diner now and see how everyone is doing. Apparently, Evelyn Hattie wants to meet me there and rave about Jackson's wonderful girlfriend and how she's revitalized her hotel." He smiled at Allison appreciatively. "We can catch up later and discuss how that all came about."

"How about I make everyone dinner tonight?" Allison offered.

"Are you sure that's not too much trouble?" he asked.

"It's no trouble at all!" she said with a smile. "Jackson and I would love to have you." Jackson watched his father walk out of the garage and shook his head. His brother leaves and his father comes home. And now he was going to have dinner with his girlfriend and his dad. Four months ago, that wouldn't have even seemed like a possibility, and now that was his life. He didn't know how he had gotten so lucky.

Later that evening, with Ed Sheeran's "Firefly" playing on the radio, Allison danced slowly in his arms. His face nestled into her neck as he hummed along to the song. He thought about how much his life had changed since Allison barged her way into his life in a pair of five-inch heels.

"You never wear heels anymore," he whispered, glancing down at her bare feet.

"They don't exactly work well at the garage." She laughed.

"Do you miss it?" he asked softly.

"My heels?" she asked.

"Your life?" he corrected.

She sighed softly against his neck. "No." He lifted his head to look at her, their eyes meeting as she smiled.

"What about the life you built in the city? Your apartment overlooking the city, full of people you enjoyed watching so much?" He swayed slowly with her to the music.

"I built a better life than I ever dreamed I could have here with you. We wake up every morning with the wind blowing through the trees. We get to take Whiskey on walks to the creek. I have a job I enjoy, people who I love being around, and a home where I feel loved." She smiled happily.

"I'm glad, Allison." He smiled and pecked his lips against her cheek. "Because I love you. All of you, even when you drink kale smoothies and bust my balls at work."

"I wouldn't have to bust your balls if you weren't an asshole all the time." She giggled as he kissed her neck, causing her to squeal. "Come on, your dad will be here soon, and I need to finish dinner."

"Fine, but what do you say after dinner, you and I take the bike out to the creek and watch the fireflies?"

He kissed her forehead, and she hummed in approval before walking over to the stove. "I'd like that," she sighed happily. "We can take a blanket and a bottle of wine, or a beer for you, if you prefer."

"Hey, now you're talking my language. A little stargazing, a lot of hanky-panky!" He smirked, sticking his finger in the tomato sauce, and tasting it.

She slapped his hand away. "I never said there was going to be hanky-panky."

"You didn't say there wasn't." He winked.

"You're impossible," she groaned, stirring the pot of spaghetti sauce.

"I certainly am, but you love me anyway." He shrugged, setting the plates out on the table.

"Yes, I do, Jackson Lancaster, yes I do."

Butterfly: A Lancaster Novel
Book 3 - Coming in October 2025

Love was a four-letter word that Dylan Lancaster despised.

Oh sure, love seemed to work out just splendidly for his sister Samantha and his best friend Blake Forrester. They'd been living in an absolute bubble of euphoria for almost a year now. And his older brother Jackson's new relationship with Allison Hanover was benefitting from a big ole case of love hysteria. But in his own life, well, Dylan Lancaster was pretty determined that love just wasn't in the cards for him.

Not that he'd been looking very hard for it. After all, he'd spent the last year falling in and out of bed with Donna Draper, Blake's ex-girlfriend. While she was hot to look at, being compared to your best friend all night long wasn't exactly on anyone's top ten list. But when you come from a small town, like Titusville, you take what you can get and for Dylan, he just wanted to fill the void sitting like a pit in the bottom of his stomach. Which made for a really unhappy and dissatisfying existence.

And he was truly unhappy. Which was how Dylan got to where he was today—sitting at his mother's gravesite, preparing for the first time in his life to leave Titusville and head to New York City.

"Well, Mom, I guess this is gonna be the last Friday visit for a while." A few leaves over his head were turning orange and falling to the ground as he looked around the cemetery.

This spot under the tree had become a place of solitude for him. Ever since Dylan had graduated high school, he had been coming up here on Fridays to visit his mom. Sometimes he would just sit on the stone bench, letting his thoughts drift idly. Other times, he would draw in his sketchbook, letting his pen distract him from the disorganized anxiety mulling about his brain. Then there were moments like today when he would just talk. Like she was still here.

He wasn't crazy. It wasn't like he ever got a response or anything. Talking to his mom was like free therapy, if he believed in that kind of crap.

"I gotta go check on Sam, just to make sure she's doing alright in the big city." So, maybe that was a bit of a fib. Sam was fine. Hell, she was probably the most adjusted of all the Lancaster siblings. He closed his eyes and inhaled. "Alright fine, you win Mom. I'm not doing alright. This last year has been bad. All the stuff with Blake, the crap with I've been doing with Donna. I'm numb. I don't even feel like myself most days, though that might be because I'm drunk most of the time," he sighed. "Who am I kidding? You probably already know all of this already." Biting back his emotions, he whispered. "Somehow you still know everything, don't you?"

A breeze caused the leaves to lift off the ground and swirl across the lot. "I've got this dark pit of sadness inside of me. I can't explain it, but something's just missing and I don't know how to find it, or if it's even out there." He leaned back on the bench and stared up at the sky. "Sam has Blake and Jax has Allison and I'm happy for them, really I am. You'd love how freaking happy they both are. It's sickening, honestly. I've never seen Jax smile this much before. It's honestly gross. I'm not gonna miss that for a few months."

He looked down at the time on his phone and realized that he needed to get going if he wanted to make it to his cab on time. "I'm gonna go to the city and figure out my shi—crap, Mom. I promise. I'm gonna make you proud of me." He placed his hand on the stone in front of him and stood, sticking his earbuds in his ears. "Bye, Mom, I promise I'll come back when I'm better."

He walked back to his bicycle, humming along to Noah Kahn's "Bad Luck" as the music came to life in his earbuds. Behind him, the small blue and green dragonfly still fluttered away at the bottom of the tree where he left it.

Afterword

Starting book two was bittersweet for me, because I thought for sure nothing could replace Sam and Blake in my heart. But as I sat down and started writing this book, I became obsessed with Jackson Lancaster and his loveable, sarcastic nature. And the more I wrote him, the more Sawyer from Lost slipped into my head. I can't even replace it now. But thank you, Josh Holloway, for being a huge inspiration for how I wrote this character. He's my baby boy, and I feel like I'm overprotective of him now.

Writing Allison was difficult for me at first because she wasn't in book one, and it took me forever to find her voice and welcome her into the family. She felt like an outsider, and I guess that worked for her because she truly was an outsider coming into this small town and even I had to fully accept her into the Lancaster family by the end.

Before this book, I thought I preferred the friends to lovers trope. After all, that's how I found my happily ever after, but Jackson and Allison quickly became a place of joy for me. With their snippy banter and sarcastic quips floating back and forth like a tennis match, they were easy to fall in love with.

Now as I step away from book two and begin work on book three (because I think Dylan deserves to find some HEA) I'm already beginning to mourn the loss of my bickering couple. Don't worry, we will hear from them again in book three! The Lancasters never truly abandon family, so expect to see the entire gang return in the last book.

As always, thanks to my family for listening to my dinner table ramblings about my fictional family who join us each night. My daughter and husband continue to offer advice and feedback on where to go with the stories and encouragement to keep writing.

My daughters, Bek and Faith, who are lucky not to have to hear this nightly and moved away to Missouri, for providing support and cheerleading from afar. Thanks for the social media boost, I'm still trying to figure this marketing stuff out!

And finally apologizes to my son, who is just trying to eat his hamburger in peace without having to hear about which brother is grumpy and which one is stubborn and, God forbid, which parts of my book are spicy. Sorry Eric!

As a final note, I have to thank my company for all the support I have gotten in my Quest to write this book. I couldn't have done it without the start from them and I feel honored to work for a company that believes in investing and nurturing the passions of their employees. And thank you to everyone who has reached out, provided a supportive word, or just acknowledged the hard work. Twenty-one years in one place and I'm still always amazed by the many people I've met and continue to meet along the way.

On to the next, Butterfly awaits, and I cannot wait to see how Dylan's story unfolds. Look out grumpy, sunshine is coming!

About the author

Stacy Goforth was born on the east coast but spent most of her young life moving from state to state and overseas with her parents. After settling in Arizona as a young adult, she found an addiction to sunshine and the ease of never needing to set her clock back again too good to be true and settled down. Now, 20-plus years later, she has grown a life with her husband, four children, one grandchild, two dogs, and two cats.

After spending the last 14 years writing fanfiction for shows like Glee, Once Upon a Time, and Bridgerton, she created The Lancasters, with Dragonfly, A Lancaster Novel, the first book in the series. To hear more about her thoughts, writing process, and book ideas, you can join her on the following social media sites:

Instagram *@stacygoforthauthor*
Tumblr: *https://stacygoforthauthor.tumblr.com/*
Facebook: *@stacygoforthauthor*
Website*: https://stacygoforthauthor.com/*

Sign up for this author's newsletter to get exclusive access to Digital Art. Joining also gets you access to other exclusive content like bonus chapters from the books, new POV chapters, and other artwork. Join by following the QR code.

Also by

Dragonfly: *A Lancaster Novel* Book 1

By: Stacy Goforth

Samantha Lancaster never thought she'd see Blake Forrester again. He was her high school crush, her unrequited first love, and her older brother's best friend. But when she returns to her hometown to help her brother recover from a motorcycle accident, she's suddenly thrust back into the world of know-it-all blonde bullies and awkward sexual tension. And to make matters worse, she can't seem to stop sticking her foot in her mouth.

Blake Forrester and Dylan Lancaster lived by a strict bro-code. But with Sam back in town, Blake can't stop thinking about her. He knows he shouldn't break the code, but the temptation is too strong. And with each passing day, the bro-code seems to become more and more complicated. Will Blake be able to resist his feelings for Sam and stay loyal to his best friend, or will the pull between them be too strong to deny?

For fans of forbidden romance and small town drama, "Dragonfly" is a must-read. With relatable characters and a steamy love story, you won't be able to put this book down.

Available on Paperback and eBook on Amazon and booksellers online.

https://books2read.com/stacygoforthauthor

Content Warnings

This book contains the following content that may be disturbing to some readers: Mention of death of a parent due to an illness (Cancer), alcohol use, sexual content, and swearing.